Born in Melbourne, Mark O'Flynn now lives in the Blue Mountains. His first novel, *Grassdogs,* was published in 2006 after winning the Harper Collins/Varuna manuscript prize. *False Start, A Memoir of things Best Forgotten* was published by Finch Publishing (2013) and his latest novel, *The Forgotten World*, by Fourth Estate/HarperCollins Australia (2013). His short stories, articles, reviews and poems have appeared in a wide range of journals and magazines both here and overseas including *Australian Book Review, The Bulletin, The Good Weekend (Sydney Morning Herald)*, *Heat, Westerly, Meanjin, Southerly, Island, Overland, New Australian Stories* (Scribe) and *Best Australian Stories* (Black Inc). Mark works as a teacher of English and ESL in a NSW prison.

# PRAISE FOR MARK O'FLYNN

## *SHORT STORIES*

### *Iago*
'It is feisty, edgy and challenging writing that works
superbly.'
—Helen Elliot, *The Age*

### *The Ping-Pong Principle*
'A perfect exemplar of the short story form... By the end...
this frame is itself blended with the story and transfigured
into a principle, a code to live by. Brilliant.'
—Matthew Lamb, *Review of Australian Fiction*

### *Beneath the Figs*
'Subtle layering of detail that seems casually incidental...
Mark O'Flynn's skilful use of tone has you smiling right up
until the story reveals its poignant underside.'
—Cate Kennedy, *The Best Australian Stories 2011*

## *GRASSDOGS*

'Mark O'Flynn paints Edgar with such sure and savage
strokes that he is the novel, and the novel is him.'
—Barry Oakley, *The Bulletin*

'The enduring image of *Grassdogs* comes with the title: a
tidal wave of dogs–mutts of all breeds and conditions –
surging through the grassland like fleas through fur, just

below the undulating blades... a lyrical literary novel...'
—Katharine England, *The Adelaide Advertiser Review*

'His writing is more than accomplished and there are
moments when it sings with the confidence of a writer in
complete control of his craft.'
—Liam Davison, *The Age*

'There is precision and muscularity in his writing; an
admirable tendency towards understatement; a pleasing
musicality; a sense of narrative shape. O'Flynn can conjure
up scenes that are almost magic-realist in their melodrama,
off-beat humour and casual grotesqueness... The closing
chapter is a minor masterpiece...'
—Chris Boyd, *Australian Book Review*

'Mark O'Flynn's novel crackles with a desperate energy...
*Grassdogs* is full of arresting imagery and unusual turns of
phrase.'
—Cameron Woodhead, *The Age*, Pick of the Week

## *FALSE START*
A Memoir of Things Best Forgotten
'... as this unreliable memoir of many things best forgotten
gathers pace, Mark O'Flynn's laconic Australian comedy
exhibits a voice and a compelling timbre of its own... The
last fifty pages of *False Start*, set in Sydney, Portugal and
Ireland, are deeply touching and utterly hilarious.'
—Ross Fitzgerald, *The Australian*

'Spiked with humour and fine observation...'
—Ross Southernwood, *Sunday Herald*

Spineless Wonders
ABN98156041888
PO Box 220 STRAWBERRY HILLS
New South Wales, Australia, 2012
www.shortaustralianstories.com.au

First published by Spineless Wonders 2013


Text copyright © Mark O'Flynn
Edited by Annie Parkinson. Layout by Bronwyn Mehan
Cover image with permission from unrestrictedstock.com
Cover design by Bettina Kaiser

Typeset in Adobe Garamond Pro
Printed and bound by Lightning Source Australia


National Library of Australia Cataloguing-in-Publication entry
White Light/Mark O'Flynn
1st ed.
978-0-9872546-2-7 (pbk.)
*A823.4*


This project has been assisted by the Australian Government through the Australia Council, its arts funding and advisory body.

for Barb and Liv and Eamon

MARK O'FLYNN


WHITE LIGHT

'Like you, I have spent most of my life baffled.'
from *What Darkness Covers*,
Tony Curtis

# CONTENTS

14    Beneath the Figs
25    Lovely Outing
33    Bulldozer
37    Loaded Dice
41    The Ingot
49    Iago
54    White Light
67    Ping-Pong Principle
75    The Isthmus
85    Bridie
96    Stealth
105   Banjo
111   A Good Break
118   Red Shoes
128   Drip, Drip, Drip
133   Tales of Action and Adventure
143   Acknowledgements

# BENEATH THE FIGS

Shona and Dean live in Abigail Street, a street that is twenty houses long on either side. It is a short, shady side-street cutting between two main roads that bludgeon their way through the suburbs away from the city. Abigail Street is cool and quiet, while at either end, especially at peak hour, there is mayhem.

The shade is the result of a row of Morton Bay figs that buckle the footpaths of Abigail Street. The trees are on death row, having been placed under a council intervention order into their longevity. These trees have proved an ideal habitat for a colony of fruit bats that each year come to feast on the ripening figs. Every night, particularly during the full moon, the bats swirl drunkenly through the sky like the opening credits of an old Vincent Price film. In daylight they hang from the trees like blackened tumours. In the words of local residents the colony has grown into a plague.

If she happens to leave it out overnight, by morning Shona's washing is a mess. Her uniforms particularly vulnerable. Dean's car is also a mess. Every car in the street is a mess. A siren is set up in order to scare the bats out of the branches with short, sharp blasts like a ferry's foghorn. It partially works. The bats fly about frantically for a while, then settle again to their gorging. Unfortunately, neighbourhood children are also woken by the sudden noise and the locals begin to see there are pros and cons to this and other solutions.

One evening, after a visit to the theatre where Steven Berkhoff tries to terrify them with dramatised tales of Edgar Allan Poe, they find themselves driving up Abigail Street at bat hour. They are everywhere. Suddenly, out of the distorted moonlight, a drunken bat falls from the sky and smacks against their windscreen. Shona screams. The bat's face is pointed, like a fox's muzzle. Its ears are sharp and, well, bat-like. Dean slams on the brakes and the bat, dribbling rabid saliva and fig juice, slides down the glass and off the bonnet, wings outstretched as if trying to hang on.

Other people have had similar experiences.

There are so many bats that their urine is starting to kill the fig trees. It looks as though the leaves, yellow and withering, have been sprayed with Agent Orange. The Botanical Gardens are apparently facing a similar problem. This is when their neighbour, Ian Ikin, contacts the council. He demands something be done about the bats. They should be sprayed with a natural solution of python excrement and shrimp paste, he says. The council demurs. Their solution comprises a proposal to get rid of all the fig trees, to pave the entire nature strip with asphalt. There is a chorus of protest.

One of Shona and Dean's neighbours is a family of Plymouth Brethren. Scarf people, the children call them, although not to their faces. They appear to have no opinion whatsoever on the problem of the bats. Dean likes to think facetiously that the bats are the agents of Satan come to test the resolve of the Brethren. On the other side are the Ikins. They are the ones who lobbied for the siren. The siren has been borrowed from a vintner friend of theirs who uses it to frighten birds from his vines. When the figs themselves come under threat the Ikins are the most vocal in defending the trees and the amenity they give to the local area. You can't underestimate, they say, the value of shade.

There is bat shit all over the footpaths of Abigail Street It stinks of sour, fermented figs. Shona has to dodge the lumps as she walks from the car to the front door. Bats squeal in the trees, hanging there like great drips of bitumen. She shivers involuntarily. The invisible whump of their wings as they flap up the street is unsettling, especially after a long night shift where she has otherwise been dealing with patients' greatest fears. Nurses often work with the human condition in extremis. Her nerves are simultaneously exhausted and frazzled. The last thing she needs is bats.

In the Ikins' house music is blaring. She wonders if she should phone, ask them to turn it down. But she doesn't. On the other side, in the Brethren house, all is dark. The Ikins and the Brethren (actually called the Braithwaites) do not get on ideologically. Shona and Dean are the meat in the sandwich. The Ikins have no children. Shona and Dean have two. The Brethren have eight. The Ikins' yard is messy with straggly native banksias, acacias and wattles. Pebble paths wind among them and they have a birdbath, empty now due to water restrictions. Ian Ikin is vocal in using his lack of ownership of a lawnmower as a measure of his carbon footprint. The Brethren's yard, by contrast, is clipped and shorn and barren. An expanse of couch lawn, bordered by a couple of pot-bound buxus shrubs. In their windows the lace curtains are never parted.

Mr Braithwaite owns a muffler repair shop in an outer suburb. Owns is perhaps the wrong word. The Plymouth Brethren (Inc.) are probably the owners and Mr Braithwaite just manages it. Dean took his car there once when it sounded as though it had a chest infection. The most unusual thing about Braithwaites' muffler shop is that they have no credit card facilities. There is no eftpos machine and no computer. There is a sign on the wall behind the receptionist's head that reads: *No cheques. Cash only.* Dean recognises the receptionist and realises that she is Braithwaite's daughter. One of the eight. He also realises that she is pregnant. Dean has to catch a taxi to the bank to withdraw the cash in order to deal with this primitive system of doing things. Do they have some religious dispensation from accepting cheques? What a crock, he thinks. They have hydraulic lifts, don't they? They have pneumatic spanners.

Later that night Dean vents his innocuous spleen to Shona over the inconvenience.

'I had to get a taxi all the way to the bank and back. You'd think they'd give me mates rates, being neighbours and all, but no.'

How dare, he wonders, they refuse to take his money?

How, Shona wonders in return, did he not know the girl was pregnant?

'It was pretty obvious once she stood up.'

'No,' Shona corrects herself, 'I meant how is it that we live next door and never even noticed? What sort of neighbours are we?'

'Ones who respect their privacy.'

Shona doubts this. She worries about the breakdown of community values, about how neighbours are becoming clusters of strangers, wary of each other.

Later she says, 'I wonder what hospital she's booked into?'

'Probably yours. That's the closest.'

'I wonder who the father is?'

'One of these other hanky-heads,' Dean says. 'There's cars pulling up there all the time.'

'I would have thought that a group like the Brethren,' says Shona, 'would be pretty vigorous about knowing who the father is.'

'Hanky-panky,' says Dean, for no other reason than it is there to be said.

Shona and Dean actually like living next door to the Brethren family. There is no noise. There is barely any sign of people living there at all. Occasionally cars do gather and people stream into the plain, Besser-bricked house and not a sound comes out. Dean has an image that the interior walls must be made of egg cartons, like the makeshift sound studios of his youth. But of course he has no idea. He has never peeped inside, though he has looked over the back fence. It is just as barren. Not even a sandpit for the kids. Isn't there something about them rejecting activities associated with fun? Fishing, for instance? Well, what are pneumatic spanners if not fun?

'I wonder which one is the grand Pooh-bah?' Dean asks one day, peering through the kitchen blinds as the cars begin to arrive.

'I don't think they have any ministerial order,' says Shona.

'Then why don't the men have to wear hankies on their heads?'

'I don't know.'

Shona is a nurse at the Prince of Wales hospital. She has just finished a stint in Oncology and a few months ago moved to Maternity. She likes the Maternity ward as it always gives her a feeling of hope. One day, she notices a young girl in the Tresillian unit. Actually it is the scarf wrapped tightly across the girl's head that makes her look twice, and she recognises one of her neighbours. The girl's shoulders are hunched forward, as if she is trying to take the weight of the smock off her breasts. Shona recalls that awful sensation. She makes some congratulatory noises but is embarrassed, not only by the girl's rejection of her interest, but because she does not know the girl's name.

'Did everything go well?' Shona asks.

'Yes, thank you.'

'Did you have to have stitches?'

'No.'

'It's just that you're here in Tresillian.'

'We're just trying to find some alternative feeding method.'

'Oh, well good luck,' says Shona, not wanting to intrude. 'And congratulations.'

'Yes. Thank you.'

Shona walks off on her sensible rubber soles thinking: I could rot in my house before this girl came in to check on me.

Without this fortuitous meeting, they would not have known there was a baby. There is no fanfare. No cots or prams or newborn paraphernalia wheeled into the bland brick house. No relentless midnight screaming. The Ikins want to take a bottle of champagne in there. By force. Shona says she does not think it would be a welcome gesture. So they drink the champagne themselves. Wetting the baby's head by proxy.

'I wonder what they've got hidden in their garage?' says Dean. 'I bet they've got fishing rods in there.'

After a few bottles they hear themselves getting a little raucous; however, from next door there comes nothing but a stony silence.

As a trial run, the council comes with a cherry picker and half-a-dozen men in hard hats with chainsaws who cut down one of the fig trees. Admittedly it is dead, but that does not stop the Ikins working the phones. The Tree Preservation Officer is called to Abigail Street and work is put on hold. He detects a small contradiction in that the residents want the grey-headed flying foxes gone, but not the habitat to which they are attracted. He'll have to think about it.

As part of her duties Shona is always pleased to be rostered on to Home Visits. It gets her off the ward. Unsurprisingly, according to the logical sequence of events, one of her visits is to the house of the Braithwaites. Maddeningly, Shona has to travel all the way in to the hospital only to be given the address right next door to her own home. She drives back happy to think that afterwards she might be able to steal a cup of tea in her own kitchen, put a load of washing on. The street looks different in the middle of the day. She cannot believe how much sky there is above her yard. Sawdust from the amputated stump of the fig tree blows across the road.

She knocks on the Braithwaites' door and it is some minutes before the lace curtains flicker and an eye peers out. More minutes before the girl, a crimson scarf tied over her head as if holding down a haystack, opens the door. Beneath her scarf, her long hair hangs free, brushed and electric down the length of her back.

She stands back and ushers Shona inside. Entering slowly, Shona lets her eyes adjust to the dimness. She blinks. She has never seen a room like it. In the main room (it can hardly be a room for lounging in) there are about thirty hardbacked chairs lined up side by side around the walls of the room. There is no other furniture. No pictures. No table. Just the rectangle of chairs. In the middle of the room on a mauve bunny-rug, like some sacrificial offering, lies the baby. There is some whispering from the far end of the room. Shona glances up to see the door quietly close. She coughs, trying to break the ice.

'You worked at the muffler shop, didn't you?'

There is a whispered snort from the far room. Shona can sense there is not a man in the building.

'How do you know?' asks the girl.

'My husband... Oh, never mind. What seems to be the problem? I saw you were in Tresillian.' Shona feels as though her voice is too loud.

'My baby won't feed properly.'

Shona can see she is young. Perhaps nineteen or twenty.

'Let's have a look.'

She goes to the tiny, swaddled bundle on the floor and kneels beside it. Carefully unwraps the soft blanket. She peers closely. She starts. The baby is yellow but not jaundiced. It looks tiny and withered, pixieish, with pointed ears and, Shona sees, a pointed muzzle. Like a bat.

'What's wrong with her?'

'They say it's something called Edwards Syndrome.'

Shona has never heard of it.

'The doctors wanted to keep her, but my mother said it was time to bring her home.'

'Edwards Syndrome?'

'It's chromosomal.'

Shona stares at the shrivelled baby, then says, 'I'm embarrassed to have to ask this, but what's your name?'

The girl balks. 'Susan.'

At that moment, the door at the far end of the room opens and the mother, Mrs Braithwaite, and two other women who look just like the mother bustle in. They all wear identical crimson scarves and ankle-length skirts. One of them holds a tray rattling with teacups. They fuss around Shona and the girl and the baby, which no one picks up.

One of the aunts (they can only be the mother's sisters) asks Shona to take a seat, any seat, over by the wall.

'Will you take tea?' asks the aunt.

'Yes I will, please.'

The aunt pours from a plain pot and for a moment that is the only sound.

'Milk?'

'Yes, please.'

A cup of tea is thrust into her hands. They sit in silence for a moment with hot cups in their laps.

'The issue,' says Mrs Braithwaite from across the room, 'is that the baby won't take the breast. It is too large for the mouth. The teat of a bottle is also too large. So what alternatives are there? We were thinking of an eyedropper. Or there is formula, and perhaps a siphon.'

'Well, premature babies need all the colostrum they can get,' Shona began.

'The baby is not premature. She went to full term. She is five weeks old.'

The baby, as Shona looks again, is small enough to hold in one hand. She has seen zucchini that are larger. The eyedropper is not such a silly idea.

'It's the chromosomes,' says Susan.

'It is not the chromosomes,' snaps Mrs Braithwaite, 'it is God's will.'

'They say she will not live past two months,' says the girl to Shona, her eyes pooling with tears.

'And so now we have brought her home,' says Mrs Braithwaite. 'Christina. To her home.'

'Is she taking any milk at all?' Shona asks.

'As soon as she takes a sip she perks it back up,' says Mrs Braithwaite.

'Your flow might be too fast for the size of her stomach. We can look at that. But really, Susan, this baby would be better looked after in the hospital.'

'Thank you for your suggestion,' says Mrs Braithwaite quickly. 'We shall consider your advice. But for the present we shall pursue the idea of the eyedropper.'

Suddenly there is a scarfed aunt on either side of Shona, helping her to her feet. One of them removes the unfinished teacup from her lap.

'But,' protests Shona.

'Thank you again,' says Mrs Braithwaite.

Shona looks at Susan, who says: 'If she goes back to hospital she'll die.'

'God will prevail,' says the aunt who has not yet spoken.

The aunts steer Shona towards the door.

'But—' Shona thinks rapidly, 'you will need a breast pump.'

'Thank you for the suggestion,' crows Mrs Braithwaite.

'Do your breasts hurt?'

Susan glares. She gives a sour little nod.

'For the mastitis, put cabbage leaves in your bra,' Shona says.

'Thank you,' trills the mother, turning to her daughter.

'This is too much,' says one of the aunts, laughing. 'Cabbage leaves!'

The other one squawks, 'Breast pump!'

Shona finds herself outside the plain, wooden door at the top of the steps. The security screen snicks behind her. The couch lawn stretches to the fence. Not a weed. Next door, her own unkempt garden seems somehow foreign from this odd angle, as if appearing in a dream. She can see inside her own dining room window. Realises that if she forgot to draw the curtains she would be plainly visible. Or that her children would be plainly visible. She walks numbly out to her car. Behind her, the lace curtains are so still they might be made of concrete. She does not even think about detouring into her own house. The washing can wait. The postman rides past on his motor scooter. He skilfully pops some letters into her box without even stopping. Shona sits in her car for a moment. There are some forms she should fill in. She is aware of the dark, sleeping shapes of the bats high in the fig trees, hanging on for grim life.

# LOVELY OUTING

A stainless steel urn bubbles away by itself on a Laminex bench. It sounds at the same time dangerous and comforting. Kevin, my son-in-law, scowls at his wristwatch; he doesn't think I should be here at all, but it's lovely to be out and about for the day. Such a gorgeous, sunny morning. The sky as bright as a postcard. I never knew how much I would miss sparrows. A nice cup of tea and my family about me. It's so long since we've all been out together.

My daughter, Jane, in her tan suit, is already dabbing her eyes with a tissue. They told us this might happen. Kevin sits on the hardbacked chair with his thick arms folded like an Easter Island statue. They're here to lend moral support, whatever that is, and I'm glad they are here, like at Christmas.

It's nice to sit with a cup of tea in a little square of sunshine. A fly butts itself against the window. Blue walls. A monsteria deliciosa in a clay pot winds its way up a little trellis towards the light. I do wish Jane would stop her snivelling. I wonder about the benefits of snivelling as a form of moral support. Mr Draper is going through his papers.

'Are you all right, Mrs Lapin?' he asks, catching my eye. He is the sort of man who seems to be wearing glasses even when he isn't.

'Of course,' I say with a smile. Why shouldn't I be all right?

We all enjoy the air's warmth. Or the breeze through the window. For our various reasons.

After a few minutes, the door opens and two big men come in. One of them must be seven feet tall at least; he has to duck beneath the portal. They are both wearing uniforms with shiny buttons and epaulettes. Then follows a smartly dressed young man whom I do not recognise but then, how could I be expected to? I barely recognise my own grandchildren. Kevin and Jane both stiffen in their seats. Kevin picks fluff from his trousers. Someone is wearing aftershave. The young man smiles at me, rather sheepishly. Surely this can't be him: Troy. No, this can't be. He looks such a nice boy.

I take time to polish my specs.

'Hello, Mrs Lapin,' he says.

A moment passes. It is clear that he has practised his manners. Mr Draper ushers him to a chair. Troy first folds his jumper over the back of it then sits. His clothes are nice and clean. And those slacks are coming back into fashion. The two men in uniform sit outside our small circle, trying to pretend they aren't really there. One of them opens a magazine. The tall one goes to the urn by the window. He actually blocks out some daylight. You can see the dust swirl in his wake.

'Well Troy,' says Mr Draper, 'I'm sure you know why we're here.'

'Yes.'

'And you're a willing participant in this process?'

'Yes. I've been looking forward to this for a long time.'

'Is this Troy?' I ask, realising suddenly that it's me they're talking about.

'Don't upset yourself, Mum,' Jane says, laying her hand on my arm.

I look at it but I do not recognise what should be so obvious to me.

'I'm not upset.'

'Yes, it's me Mrs Lapin,' says the young man.

'Is it, Mr Draper?'

Mr Draper nods encouragingly. The urn boils.

'No. This nice-looking young man can't be the one who attacked me. No.'

'I'm afraid that he is,' says Mr Draper.

'He doesn't always look this clean,' pipes up the giant from the coffee urn.

He is so big I wonder how we could possibly be of the same species.

Kevin's foot is tapping rapidly, one leg folded across the other knee. The giant carries a Styrofoam cup of tea as if it is a flake of apple across to his friend. Mr Draper continues: 'I understand that this is difficult. We're here to acknowledge what Troy has done to Mrs Lapin, to offer amends and to make restoration for the events that took place two and a half years ago. We are also here for Mrs Lapin to state how significantly these events have affected her over time. Mrs Lapin, would you like to begin?'

Me? Now? I don't know what to think. 'Well, I can't believe that this is the same young man. Look how nicely he's dressed. And he's even gone to the effort to iron his slacks.'

'He's scum.'

'It's more effort than you've gone to, Kevin.'

'Mum,' says Jane, 'don't be fooled by appearances.'

Scum and appearances fill my eyes. There is a sunny pause. Clink of cups. Lovely.

I feel that before too long I would like to visit the lavatory.

'Mrs Lapin,' a voice speaks. It's Troy. 'I know I've done the wrong thing. I'm really not that sort of person. I know I've caused you pain. And I'm sorry.'

'Excuse me, Troy,' Mr Draper interrupts. 'It doesn't help anyone if you're going to gloss over everything. You need to itemise each act for which you are responsible and for which you are ultimately sorry. The function of this conference is to facilitate that process. Otherwise we're all wasting our time.'

'I'd like him to understand,' Jane squeaks, always the first to get in her penny's worth. 'I'd like him to know not just what pain he put my mother through, but also everyone else, me in particular. I was the one who had to take extended leave from my job. I took her to the hospital every day. I want him to appreciate that I was the one who had to watch the pain she went through in rehab. I was—'

'For goodness sake,' I say. 'It was only my shoulder.'

Troy stares at the bitten nails at the ends of his fingers. Mr Draper suggests that we all calm down. Have some more tea. The fly still skates across the glass of the window. Beyond I can see some sails on the water. Mr Draper helps us to resume. He's very good at this *it's the principle* sort of thing.

'I understand the emotional pain and the... in-con-ven-ience I put you through, Mrs Mitchell,' says Troy. 'And I'm sorry for that too—'

'How does he know my name?' Jane says.

Kevin and Mr Draper shrug. They look at me as if I have the answer.

'Well... yes. I, er... yes, I wrote to him, Jane. And yes, I told him about us.'

'You wrote to him?' says Kevin.

'You told him about us?' says Jane.

'Does he know our address?' asks Kevin suddenly.

'I told him about our family. About Christmas.'

'Why, for God's sake?' Kevin snorts.

'He asked. And no one else writes to me. It was polite.'

All the cups are empty. Mr Draper intervenes at this point —at last someone backing me up.

'That's correct, Mr Mitchell. Written contact must be established between the victim and the perpetrator before the proper process of restorative justice can be instigated. All your mother-in-law's letters were fully monitored.'

'You read my mail?' I squawk. Kevin looks much happier. 'Troy, did you know that?'

Troy nods. Such a sweet face. Hard to imagine.

'Do you have anything you'd like to ask of Troy, Mrs Lapin?'

'One thing I have always wanted to know, Troy, is why you so betrayed my trust that day?'

'Mrs Lapin,' he says at last, 'I'm sorry that I picked you out of the crowd. To be my victim. I picked you because I could see... I could see you were vulnerable. I'm sorry I let you take my arm. And that, I betrayed your trust.'

'You helped me across the road. You were a gentleman.'

'I never meant to hurt you. I'm sorry that I snatched your bag and you fell to the ground.'

At this point Jane interrupts again. 'He's glossing over the part where he dragged her along the street until the strap broke. He doesn't know about the bruises and abrasions. I do. I know all about that, the blood on her stockings, I can't get that out of my head.'

'I held on tight, didn't I, for an old girl?'

'Yes, you did,' says Troy, his face Christmas white. 'I'm sorry that you dislocated your shoulder.'

'Yes, that hurt. But not as much as you betraying my trust.'

It's almost as if I don't remember the things he is speaking of—as if they happened long ago to someone else. Well, it was long ago, but that shouldn't make any difference. It's true—my trust has been betrayed and broken.

'I didn't mean for any of that to happen. If I could take everything back I would. But I can't. I have to live with who I am. I'm also sorry that I was... addicted to drugs and my addiction made me do those things. To you.'

'It was drugs that made you say those things?'

'Yes.'

'That'd be right,' says Kevin, 'nothing but a despicable junkie.'

I can't believe how rude he is being. There is a satisfied silence from the officers. Troy ignores them. Mr Draper directs traffic, asking Kevin to calm down, etcetera.

Everyone takes a deep breath.

'I'm sorry for the shame and hurt I caused you. I know you had to stop playing bowls when you were very active.' Tears suddenly leak from Troy's eyes. 'I'm sorry for the pain I caused my own parents—they don't want to have anything more to do with me.'

'No, really? A granny-basher?' says Kevin sardonically.

'Oh, be quiet, Kevin.'

'I'm sorry for just about... everything.'

'Boo hoo hoo,' sobs Jane in her shrill starling's voice. It pulls me up short. One of the guards snickers. I am shocked to realise what I have never seen before, that my daughter is a nasty person.

Kevin asks a pointed question: 'Is it true that you were raped in jail?'

'Yes, that's true.'

'And I bet that's another thing you're sorry about.'

Troy lets his tears fall. He cannot hide them anywhere. I cannot believe the rudeness of my family. One of the officers sitting outside the circle yawns loudly, crushing his Styrofoam cup.

'Well, I'm not sorry.'

Kevin and Jane both splutter. Some tea spills.

'Oh, I am sorry that my shoulder was hurt, and I'm sorry that I had to give up playing bowls, but I'm not sorry that this nice young gentleman offered to help me. I didn't know how I was going to get across that busy road.'

'Jesus Christ,' Kevin groans.

'And I'm not sorry that meeting you, Troy, has meant that I've been able to come on this lovely trip to town. I would never have done that otherwise. It's been so long since I spent such time with my family.'

Everyone's eyes follow a different fly, not knowing where to rest. We chat for a little longer. Kevin gets a few things off his chest. More tea is drunk. When I eventually come back from the lavatory, Mr Draper makes Troy promise that he will stay off drugs, and that he will always have clean urine, which is something I do not wish to understand. He agrees to my request that he writes regularly to let me know the state of his drug-free progress. The officers, Troy and Mr Draper sign some papers. We say our goodbyes and Troy kisses my hand. I believe I almost blush. I see the officers put handcuffs on his wrists as they lead him out. He looks so small alongside them. He gives me a wink. Jane escorts me down in the lift. I amble on my stick and her elbow, which feels like cardboard.

When we reach the bottom, Kevin strides ahead to fetch the car. The afternoon has melted and clouded over. The sky has faded. My shoulder is throbbing.

* * *

I sit in the passenger seat. Jane and Kevin's muffled argument comes to me through the window as they dawdle on the footpath. She has things to pick up from the shops. Kevin will get a taxi. My daughter will drive me home and she will leave me there with my pot plants. I wonder when she'll bring my grandchildren to visit again? There's only so much wondering that can be given to that subject.

I want so much to read the next letter Troy will send.

* * *

I am happy when the letter arrives. I see again that he is not a very good speller. He tells me how happy he was to finally meet me at the conference, how much it meant to him to see me and to say the things he had to say before he—y'know — ran out of steam and that afterwards, driving back to prison where he will serve the remainder of his sentence, the guards had stopped at some traffic lights where, winding down the window an inch, he could smell the sea.

# BULLDOZER

This is my story about the bulldozer. I reckon they're awesome. Not like my brother's little toy ones mucking about in the sandpit. But real, monstrous, dirty big bulldozers with gears and cogs and that caterpillar tread that would smash your bones to smithereens if you stood in its way. One is building a road up past our house.

I wish my dad would buy a bulldozer. I could keep it in the backyard and play on it.

In my backyard is a Hills Hoist squealing slowly in the breeze like a buckled windmill. Its arms are crooked from too much swinging, although I think it's because the washing is too heavy. That is all I want to say about my backyard.

A bulldozer wouldn't really fit in it.

The bulldozer parks each day on the hill near our house. And a grader. And a steamroller, with a big, shiny wheel like a rolling pin. They are making the road.

At the bottom of the hill is the 'bush'. It is not really the bush but it is called the bush because it is bushy. There is a creek with tadpoles in it. At the end of the bush the creek and the tadpoles go down a pipe. If you catch them in a jar then hold them up to the light you can see the veins in their tails. If you pour them on the ground they wriggle. Then they stop wriggling and are boring.

The bulldozer at the top of the hill has brown grease oozing out of its axles. It is orange. Orange is my favourite colour because that is the colour of bulldozers. Its blade is cold and smooth. On weekends, kids climb on the bulldozer and muck around. They pretend to drive it and make engine noises. I have to stretch so far to reach the pedals my legs hurt.

We watch the bulldozer making the road from the top of the hill. A brown man with muscles like a frog pulls the levers. There is another hill made of clay pushed aside by the bulldozer. From the top you can see and smell new houses.

One morning before Sunday school I get up early and put on my best dress. I race up the road for a quick muck around on the hill. There is no one else there and I am kind of invisible. I climb aboard my bulldozer. It smells sweet of grease and oil. I push knobs, pull levers, turn the wheel, stretch for pedals, make engine noises with my mouth, when—CLUNK— something goes clunk. It is moving. It is alive. I jump to the ground. I watch my bulldozer roll, slowly at first, then faster, down hill and over—oh, did I forget to mention the embankment?—over the embankment. My bulldozer does a few cartwheels. After a while there is peace and quiet. I look over the edge of the embankment. The bulldozer is on its back where the tadpoles were. It looks dead, all mangled and still.

There is mud on my dress. I run for it. Down the road, through my back door, into my room. If anyone sees my dirty dress, I'll cop it. They will put two and two together and I will go to jail. Even when I stop running, my heart is still catching up. I hide my dirty dress in the bottom of the wardrobe. Put on my pyjamas. Get into bed. Snore a bit.

After a while my father yells for us to all get up and get dressed for Sunday school.

'Come on, no dawdling now.'

My heart starts running again. I get up and find a nice clean dress. I yawn a lot. Luckily my hair is still tousled. No one knows that I am a criminal. I eat two breakfasts.

'Righto you lot, in the car,' my father yells. 'And no fiddling.'

He likes to yell. It gets us going. My brother and I fight for the front seat. I win. I fiddle. Fiddle with the buttons, push, pull, squirt water on the windscreen, honk the horn, turn the wheel, honk the horn. By accident, I pull the lever with a spring in it. The lever goes down. Something goes clunk again. It looks like I have not learnt my lesson. Dad yells. I look up. The house is moving. I am rolling backwards. Dad is running alongside the car. He opens the door. He looks funny as he hops on one leg. He falls in and stamps on the brake as if he is killing a spider. I get a clip over the ear but that is fair. I have to sit in the back seat. My ear stays hot.

After a few days everyone has forgotten about the bulldozer.

I grow up a bit.


Then there is a man in a suit at the front door mumbling to my mother.

'Jennifer, come here please,' she calls.

She never says please. This means I am going to jail now. I tell the man the truth. Yes, I sometimes play on the big machines, so do all the other kids. My favourite is the grader.

No, I never played there on Sunday morning. No, I don't know how the bulldozer got in the bush at the bottom of the hill. The man says a word. He says, 'Liar.' I cry. This makes my mum mad. She says, 'Jennifer was with us at church last Sunday morning, as she is every week. It could have been any of the neighbourhood children. How dare you accuse… she would never…'

Her voice sounds like iron filings. I am a magnet.

The man leaves with his red face. His tyres go squeak on the road. My mum wins. I go into the backyard to swing on the washing line and be invisible for a while. I notice my Sunday school dress flapping there with no mud on it.

We are eating dinner. Mum and Dad are having a serious chat. I hide my broccoli under some lettuce. I look up once or twice and watch my dad putting two and two and two together. He glares at the salt. My brother kicks me under the table. This time I let him. I wonder when the man in the suit will come back to take me to jail. I hear Dad say they are going to build new houses down the bush when the road is finished. I want to say something like where will the tadpoles live? But it is better to keep quiet. There is no dessert. That is fair.

No one in our house ever mentions the bulldozer again.

# LOADED DICE

An incidental character in a story by Morris Lurie is said to have undertaken a thesis on the popular board game, *Monopoly*. I find this disturbing, how life can imitate fiction, because I myself have recently completed such an exegesis and, finding little of academic or theoretical interest in the literature, was under the misapprehension that I was doing original research. Not so, it seems. Lurie has pipped me at the post.

*Monopoly*. It is an intriguing topic. Personally, I take something of an analytical approach to the psychosocial metaphors of the game. Let us say, for example, that I am the Boot and you are the Racing Car. Nothing odd there. I like boots. And you? You start. After our preliminary circumnambulation of the board, you throw a three plus a five. Euston Road. You buy. I throw a one and a three. Income Tax. Ten percent. I do not mind. Your turn will come. Resign yourself; sooner or later everyone has to pay income tax. Your next throw of the dice adds up to five. Whitehall. You buy. I have no anecdote concerning Whitehall. My turn. The dice feel light as a pair of wren's eggs in my hand. At first glance, they seem to display a veritable bevy of dots. Nine. Whitehall. I pay the rent. Your Racing Car accelerates to the wishing well of the Community Chest. You draw a card: Advance to Mayfair. Whacko, you crow. And slap down the cash. My boot plods its way to Free Parking. No joy there. Just tyre marks on the road and broken glass in the gutter. You collect two hundred dollars as you pass Go and promptly invest it in the acquisition of a railway station. Surely you can do no worse than the current government. At the opposite end of the defined world I land on Fenchurch but I am a more selective investor and choose not to purchase. I see myself operating at the more up-market end of the spectrum, which may explain my pique at Mayfair.

With a six, you snap up Pall Mall. I tell you the story of how once, when visiting the real Pall Mall, a young English waif begged me for money to buy chips. Instead, I offered her an apple, which she threw at my head. Interesting? No. My go. Oh. I throw a five and as a consequence, I land and am sent, of all places, directly to jail You throw a mere three and are thus in the position of being able to purchase Northumberland Avenue. You do. And place a house on each limb of this purple tri-unity.

Rather than pay the fine, I declare a penchant for chancing my arm. Call me wild, call me reckless but I hope to throw a double and therefore get out of jail free. I do not. Next, you buy The Strand. I throw a one and six. You buy Fenchurch. I throw a six and twirling two. Time enough to mend my broken spectacles with an old Band-Aid. You buy Piccadilly, with all its pigeons. I note, with some satisfaction, your cash flow is looking a bit thin. It's the old boom and bust cycle. I pay the fine. You see how in the brief interlude while I have been languishing on remand, possessing little more than the wits I was born with, you have turned into an all-devouring property mogul. An enemy of the people. You own, let's list them: two railway stations, Euston Road, Whitehall, Pall Mall, Northumberland Avenue, The Strand, Piccadilly and Mayfair. Already a widening social rift has split the good nature and sense of trust that was originally between us. Healthy competition gone sour. I contemplate stealing from the Bank, but Durkheim (is it?) says this is a natural response after a period of incarceration.

On my release from prison, I land on one of your estates (with attendant development in progress). An outlandish price at this end of the property market. I remember when the neighbourhood amounted to little more than a pile of beans. I still have enough floating capital to pay the rent. From my share of the general booty of $15,140 I have remained a model of frugality. However, I now hate you. I want to vandalise all your innocent suits. I want to break your windows, smash your crockery, poison your pets.

The game proceeds. The night is long. Your tycoon's empire expands. In my poverty, I plot my leap-frogging way around the board, pausing clumsily on the refuge islands of Chance and Community Chest. I have become a burden on society. A threat to your peace of mind. You move me on. My one simple ambition: to return to my roots, to scrimp and save enough to put a down payment on Old Kent Road, and perhaps a new pair of glasses. Thus, from humble beginnings. But the vicissitudes of life are not so simple. Social justice is a myth. Eventually, I bow to my recidivist nature and return to jail. Safe. Once in jug, I plot and plan. You think I am being defeatist. I do acknowledge the point, however, that this game is called *Monopoly* and not *Social Rift*. On we go unto our needle's eye.

Thus you can see the subtle analogies that a game of chance affords the dedicated student. Such a wealth of material cannot be ignored in the cause of research. The poetry of loaded dice and chance. Genetic predisposition versus social engineering. Such issues imply some point of comparison, even bequeath meaning.

Let me add as a postscript, that, at the conclusion of my research and upon the submission of my thesis (which I pray will be published by Routledge at the turn of the decade) I ran from the faculty office screeching for joy and for liberty. I flung my *Monopoly* board from the nearest balcony, not caring who it struck. Paper money drifting on the wind. Red hotels raining down. The game is over, the exegesis is over, welcome the jubilant freedom of ruin.

# THE INGOT

When I was much littler than I am now, our hot water system blew up and the house filled with steam. I thought a car had crashed into the house, the noise of it was that loud. You couldn't even see the walls. Hot rain dripped off the ceiling as the water went everywhere, gushing out of a broken pipe, drenching the clothes hanging off the backs of chairs.

Mum ran around bumping into things, yelling, 'Jayden, Bianca, wake up. Get out of the house.'

The lights still worked and, when we got out of bed, it was like wandering around in a warm fog. Mum looked like a soggy ghost coming out of the mist.

When she realised that a car hadn't crashed through the house and that the hot water system had blown up, she sat down on the floor with Bianca in her arms and cried. It was just one more thing. Dad, Bianca getting measles, something about a pink slip and some big bills and now this. It was too much. I opened a window to let the steam out. Piss off steam.

After the mist cleared and things began to dry out, Dad came round to dismantle the hot water service. That's what he called it—dismantling. The big tank looked like a robot dead in the front yard with all its innards stripped out. I crawled through it, where every noise echoed like a metal cave. I asked Dad if he would like to be invited in for dinner but he didn't say anything, just looked at the grease on his hands. Mum didn't say anything either, staring at us through the flywire of the front door. Then I asked him why he didn't want to live with us anymore.

'I can't answer that at the moment, Jayden,' he said. 'I have to get home.'

He packed up his tools and chucked them in the boot of his boss's car that he had borrowed, gunned the engine and took off. Home was a single room in the Family Hotel. It was a rough and scary place. Once, shots were fired through the windows from a real gun. The police were always being called. We hurried past there, walking to and from school. I always checked the windows for bullet holes. It was called the Family Hotel but we never saw too many families hanging about. Mum called it the Manson Family Hotel but I don't understand that. No one really felt like walking into the dingy dusk of the front bar to see how Dad was getting on. It was too depressing. And smelly.

He did not come back to pick up the tank, so we used it as a cubby house and a tunnel and a musical instrument that made a loud clanging noise like a copper bell when you whacked it with a broom handle. I broke the broom handle. That was one more thing also.

After the hot water tank blew up, Mum went to bed and stayed there for six days. I had to pour Corn Flakes out for me and Bianca for our dinner. Mum didn't eat much but then after a while she came good and cooked up a storm, even if she did stay in her pyjamas. Mashed potato and lemon delicious pudding with our own lemons. Things began to feel a bit better. It all had to do with money, she said, that's all. I offered her my pocket money although I was saving for a booster pack of *Yu-Gi-Oh!* cards, but she said she couldn't accept it. Whew.

I thought if I could find a treasure, then Mum would be happy and we could buy a pink slip and all that other stuff she wanted. I went out into the backyard and dug a hole underneath the clothesline to look for gold. I didn't find any, even though I wished so hard and it wasn't even for me, but for Mum. I wanted to yell out *Eureka!* and throw my hat in the air. But first I would have to find my hat. I dug and I dug. The hole was deep enough to jump into and crouch beneath the surface of the earth. The ground so dry it was like baby powder. There were no worms, and no gold. All that happened was that Mum got cranky because she nearly fell into the hole when she was hanging out the washing.

Then the electricity was cut off, so it didn't matter if we had a hot water system or not. To wash us, she would use cold water and a flannel so rough it felt like sandpaper. Flannel is a funny word, like a girl's name. Living in candle-light was an adventure, for a while. Mum dragged us to the Social Security office and encouraged us to run around and muck up so they would serve her sooner and get rid of us. It didn't work. Everyone there looked miserable and we had to wait ages.

We left with nothing—*Diddley squat*—Mum called it, although I think it was probably too much to expect them to hand over a new hot water service. We couldn't have carried it anyway, judging by the size of the old one in our front yard. On the way home, pushing the stroller with Bianca in it up the big hill, Mum started crying again. I wished so hard she would stop. I helped push the stroller. She cried as we passed all the shops, as we crossed the crossing and especially as we passed the Family Hotel and the used car lot next door. I couldn't see any bullet holes. As we were passing the bad smells coming out of the door, hoping no one would call out, I spotted something. Something shiny, just sitting there on the footpath near a *No Parking Any Time* sign. I let go of Mum's hand and picked it up. Mum continued on with the stroller, blubbering tears and snot. I caught up.

'Mum, what's this?' I held out my hand.

Her blubbering stopped. Slowly her hand closed over mine and she turned her head and kept walking, dragging me after her. Bianca was asleep in the stroller.

At home, we examined it like scientists. It was a gold ingot, Mum said. I got out my Super Sleuth magnifying glass and after we saw our giant fingerprints, we saw it had 2.5 oz stamped on the bottom of the little golden cube. We stared at it. No one asked where it came from or how it got there on the footpath, or whose it was. We just stared at it. For a few months, Mum was really happy.

\*\*\*

So I took Bianca and Jayden to the city by train. It was an adventure for them to sit up looking out the windows, or playing hide-and-seek between the back-to-back seats. They examined every new passenger who got on. Let me say that, apart from keeping my eye on the kids, at no stage did my thoughts wander from the strange miracle of the ingot in my pocket, sitting with my keys and a tissue and a packet of lifesavers. A beautiful word—ingot. Bullion is another lovely word. I'd had to make certain my pockets did not have any holes. I could not bring myself to put it in a handbag in case it was snatched by someone.

A small part of me wondered where the ingot had come from, but only a very small part. Smaller still, the civic voice that told me to hand it in as lost property and hope for a reward. That was plan B. It's nice to have a plan. I suspect the ingot had more to do with the shots and the police that the Family Hotel attracted or maybe the used car lot next door. Or both. Or nothing. What on earth would something like that be doing sitting on the street? One of those little imponderables of the world, really. Like my father leaving home when I was nineteen. Not for any reason that I could see. I don't have a clear understanding of his relationship with my mother but they always gave the appearance of being happy. I can clearly remember the last words I ever heard him speak. They were: 'Can you move your car?'

I only hope the children's father doesn't say anything so cruel.

'Mum, what's this?'

I'll never forget the sight of it when Jayden opened his palm and held it up to me. It was like a lightning bolt. I knew instantly what it was, even though I'd only ever seen gold on television before. We kept it in the sugar bowl. A bit bigger than a die or is it dice? I can never tell. One morning I woke up early to find Jayden sitting at the table weighing it in his hand. Intermingled with my pride in him was a feeling of uneasiness. I made a cup of tea and we sat in bed trying not to talk about it.

'It's not that important,' I said, really believing it.

Inside the Gold Exchange, a bundle of nerves, I approached the counter. Fifteen long steps from the door. The woman there, a proper Madam in a suit with gold cuff links, looked me up and down without changing her expression. Disdain.

'Yes?'

'I'd like to exchange some gold.'

'Indeed,' said Madam, glancing at my jeans. 'Show me the ring.'

It wasn't a question. Already she was looking elsewhere. Bitch. Jayden's nose left a smear on a glass display cabinet. Good.

'It's not a ring. It's bullion.'

'Oh.'

Her temperament changed immediately. She directed me to a gentleman at the end of a long counter.

He was perched on a pedestal, owlish behind a tall walnut desk like a judge's bench. I don't really know if it was a walnut desk, I just like the sound of it. Walnut. Ingot. Bullion. My knees were trembling and I badly wanted to wee. I had to reach up like a schoolgirl to hand it to him.

His eyebrows barely reacted. He inserted his little eyepiece into his socket and studied it. Nodding to himself. Saying 'Mmm.' Saying he'd be back in a moment. His chair squeaked.

'Where's he taking it?' Jayden asked. 'Is he stealing it?'

'It's all right. He'll bring it back.'

I was petrified. Any minute I half expected the police to burst in and arrest me. At this point Bianca loudly filled her nappy.

When he returned he held an envelope.

'At today's market value, Madam, if you wish to proceed beyond an evaluation, this item would be redeemable for—.'

He handed me the envelope with a figure written on the front.

I almost fainted.

*$2 680*

I opened the envelope. Cash. Holy… I turned to leave.

'Excuse me.'

My heart jumped. My bladder bursting.

'Yes,' I squeaked, 'I suppose you want to know where I got it from?'

'Er, no, madam. I was speaking to my colleague.'

And he was. The stuck-up bitch down the other end looked up from polishing her cuff links. None of my business.

So we left. No questions asked. Outside the exchange, the delirious chaos of Martin Place, with the lunchtime lawyers and business people eating their sandwiches and feeding the pigeons.

Jayden tugged at my arm. 'What are we going to do with my money?'

Hmm. It was his after all. He understood precisely both the letter and the spirit of the law of finders keepers. There were plenty of lawyers around to explain it if I didn't.

Shopping. We had a bang-up lunch. Chips and sauce for Bianca. Gourmet sandwiches for us. I did not get cross when Jayden couldn't finish his and threw his crusts on the floor. Then he bought a soft toy for his sister, a rhinoceros and 'something for you, Mum'. I chose a silk top with a Chinese pattern from DJs. He wanted to buy me a pink slip too, but I told him I had nothing to wear it under. Plus he bought a new booster pack of *Yu-Gi-Oh!* cards, the significance of which I don't pretend to appreciate. He also wanted a new bicycle, but I told him it would be too difficult to carry. We'll get one at home. I could see the money happily disappearing, and why not? It wasn't ours. It was probably cursed.

We wandered the street, drifting in and out of shops. It was a different experience from the usual window daydreams.

'Do you know what would make me really happy?'

'What's that, Jay?'

'A hot bath.'

Our legs were exhausted. I turned the stroller with its wonky wheel, heading towards the station.

'Are you happy, Mum?' he asked.

'I don't know. I've had a nice day.'

'You don't know if you're happy or not?'

He sounded shocked, so I smiled tiredly and gave a little shrug.

# IAGO

From this time forth I never will speak word… Sure, I said that, or something like it, it was all written down in a hurry you have to remember, but I didn't mean it. A chatterbox like me, how can you keep us quiet? I was under duress. Of course it looked bad, blood on the sword and all that, but it was all what they call circumstantial. I only remained silent on the grounds that I might otherwise incriminate myself. Let's let the smoke clear first. I can play that game. I didn't want to be stitched up with hearsay before the Duke's ambassadors and henchmen arrived. Sure, it wasn't a pretty scene, as I said, the girl dead on the bed, the Moor a-gurgle on the floor, all that claret on the carpet. My good lady wife squawking in the wings. Your Honour—these histrionics, I pray you. Well, in my defence—and I'm saying nothing that I wouldn't say to the honourable magistrate himself—I didn't kill them. It wasn't my knife. I was off drinking sack with Cassio and mighty fine sack it was too. Plenty of eyewitnesses to confirm that. I didn't even know he had a knife, though I probably could have guessed, this being good old Elizabethan bloody guts-and-thunder and all that. We've all got knives. It was, as they say, a hostage situation. You wouldn't expect him to jump off a cliff if I told him to either, but there you go. Stranger things have happened. Sure, I admit I played a few tricks on the gullible from time to time—sending the blind down dark alleys, spiking wedding firkins with my spiky spike and so on. Okay, okay, if you like, a few diabolical tricks. I don't back away from that. You know what you know. Who doesn't enjoy a harmless practical jest? The look on old mate's face when he saw the kerchief. How was I to know he would take things so seriously? Sure, I'm a comedian. In my day job I'm a fool down at the Rose, juggling my heart out, stilt-walking, balancing cats and pigeons on my head. I never said I was what I seemed. In fact, I said the opposite, if anyone was listening. I'm a chameleon. I should have been promoted to the main role, centre-bloody-stage, not the lemony face of this mordant, cloven-hoofed, left-handed villain I've been made out to be. That is a scurrilous slander upon my good name and robs from me what makes them piss poor indeed, the rogues. Unfairly tarnished, that's what I am. I reject the imputation that I am not of character impeccable: immediate jewel of my soul, etcetera. After all, my name is money. Big box office bucks. And I've followed my own advice, the good stuff I gave Roderigo, and put money in my calfskin purse. A damn sight more money they stood to make too if they'd've put my name centre stage, with supporting roles going to old holier-than-thou Othello and dizzy Desdemona. She was a good sort, luscious as a locust, and I wouldn't have minded a bit of carnal sting with her if she'd've given me half a start, making the bouncing two-backed beast, o yeah, o yeah—must say I haven't lost the old turn of phrase, have I, me lud? And you think I'm really going to hold my tongue?

Forceps or no? Picture them in the cot, prime as goats, as hot as monkeys, as salt as wolves in pride, going like a gong in a storm. Going Hell For Leather! Me lud, from whence does a phrase like that come? One can only imagine. But no, she was too pure in soul, too chaste for words. Saving her honour for him, off at the wars, when everyone else was rutting to their heart's content b'hind closed doors back here in Venice. A pox on 'em. Funny how the opening gambit allows *Venice: A street*—I would have thought more like: *Venice: A bridge o'er a stinking scum ridden drain* would have been more aptly apt. Old Wally Shackpears, my nemesis, never set foot in the place. Excellent word that, rutting. Please don't think that I'm raving. If you want raving just bring out the red hot pokers and I'll oblige. Infidelity is the name of the game, sister; or a stageboy on the side dressed up in harlotry, which is not to my taste, but in these times perhaps the judicious axe might be swung with a little more circumspect abandon. Who am I to pass judgement? Not my taste. Neither was marriage to Emilia, if truth be told, and I am honest Iago. Is that a surname or Christian name? I never hath decided. No point trying to resurrect the compact of marriage now. Had a tongue on her like a swarming vespiary and an appetite capacious enough to leave me well for dead, the villainous whore. I confess I'm not man enough for that job. Forsooth. I never understood the old boy's green-eyed gnashing and wailing. Well off out of it, I thought. Take thy money in thy slipper and scamper. All that fuss over a lost snot rag. Get over it. Embrown thy pride. Any road, a pity to see the dame blue as a berry like that on the bed. All akimbo, if that's a word allowable in the thrust and parry. A marionette. Told you I was the jocular lad. Nice-looking sort—such a waste. All the fault of this so-called permissive society; the new world condoning

old abhorrences such as mixed marriage, threesomes, fore-
skins, migrants and refugees intermingling with the rest
of us. You wouldn't read about it, though no one bothers
much about reading hereabouts, the empire writing back to
back—if you know what I mean. Don't think I'm trying to
get off the tract, but it's all designed to obfusconstumble us.
Even if some of them do have a little talent in the honest-
job-and-wife-taking-market. Without my office and without
my good name, whence do I hence? What did diplomacy
and good leadership achieve? Jealous as a coot, and now get a
load of him, with a bone-handled dagger sticking out of his
gullet. Blub, blub, blub. Who's the clever dick now? Eleven
soliloquies and still they shove me—me!—out to the wings
behind an arras and cast the very title of our play, the whole
catastrophe, to that Elizabethan clothes horse. What else
did the sweet dame see in him? I'm only saying what everybody thinks for I am, as ever, honest Iago, am I not? With a
purse full of money so as to reimburse my trusted Queen's
Counsel, for with a little honest pressing of the flesh I think
I can beat this rap. Bail, probably. Extradition to a friendly
Dukedom. Assassination of witnesses. Slow boat to exile. I'm
looking at scott free. And if I can't? Well, even when they
come for me, the Duke's executioners, with their strappado
and other torments to ope my lips, I'll ope all right. I'll sing
like a jaybird, like a fat mocking canary, any old thing that
you'd like to hear from the shadows of my castle keep. And
when they raise the glinting sunlight of their axes, I won't
keep shut. I'll fill the air with the music of my crowing. They
won't forget me in a hurry. It's just that the scribe stopped
writing it down. [*Mounts the scaffold*]. I'll rail at them from
the dock and from the condemned cell and from the bloody
basket thick with flies. I won't be silent. I'll have my final

say. I'll shout from my perch on the pike as the jackdaws strike my eyes. And when they stop my mouth with a pillow, like old mate did to Desdemona, the words will back up in my throat—back up and gurgle out my windpipe in a new language, pink bubbles with a newborn word in each, floating into the lazy air, filling their ears, if ever I did dream of such a matter. Make me shut up, I'd like to see them try…

# WHITE LIGHT

### 1.

I never received a Christmas present in my life until I met Troy Cole. Nor a birthday present for that matter but it's Christmas that really irks me. My mum believed in Jehovah. Christmas was for Satan worshippers. Last year, she used to twitch and jump all over the floor of the Hall, the armpits of her dress wet, while I sat on the hard, straight-backed chairs nursing her handbag. They said she was a little bit too fervent, because Witnesses don't twitch. In the end we tried to run away, but they tracked us down and hauled us back into the arms of Jehovah.

### 2.

Troy didn't believe in Jehovah, although he pretended he did. I was eighteen when Troy gave me my first Christmas present. It was a necklace. I loved it. When he placed it around my throat and did up the clasp with his cool fingers I felt a shiver of white light fizz through me. Later he gave me rings and bracelets and left little doodads all over my room—ribbons and small soft toys with big eyes holding signs that said *I love you*. I had to hide them in a cardboard box in the bottom of my cupboard in case someone from the Company saw them and decided they represented too much worldly involvement.

Troy had nowhere to live. He slept in bus shelters. That's where we met. I was catching a bus to Toongabbie and he was just waking up. He asked if I had an orange, and luckily I did. He sucked the juice from the pith and showed me what was in his backpack. It was a DVD player. There had never been one in our house before. Then I thought, it's only a bit of tin, what's so evil about that? So I touched it.

After a while Mum let him move in. She wanted me to meet people. Even if they were pagan. She saw straight away how much we loved each other. She never claimed to be the most devout Jehovah's Witness but she tried. She was never the best sort of Shaker either. Just as she was never the best sort of Scientologist or Plymouth Brethren.

### 3.

For someone who slept in bus shelters, Troy always seemed to have plenty of money. And a high turnover of electrical goods. He bought us things. He replaced our old broken-down vacuum cleaner with a new supersonic one. He paid off Mum's car, a sporty blue Mazda and brought home a plasma screen TV. We would sit around with our feet on the coffee table watching the game shows. He bought champagne and we giggled as we drank it.

'This is the life,' Mum would say, guiltily.

'You bet, girls,' said Troy with a big burp.

I would feel happy for being treated like an adult, and Mum would feel happy for being made to feel younger than she actually was. Then, inevitably, she would grow restless, as if the eye of God were glaring at her.

'Can't sit around all day. Idle hands and all that. This is not the truth that leads to eternal life.' She would leave Troy and me on the couch with the indentations of her bones between us.

4.

At the Kingdom Hall, the Pioneer took Mum aside and I overheard him ask, 'What does he do, this boyfriend?'

(You can never keep a secret from the Witnesses.)

'He works nights,' said Mum.

'Doing what?'

'Oh, a little of this and a little of that.'

'Is he a Catholic?'

'No, no, nothing of the sort. He's very independent.'

'Satan is the invisible ruler of the world, Elaine.'

'I know, I know. Terrible people.'

'Sharon is at an impressionable age.'

'Sharon is a good girl.'

'Without a father to guide and instruct her.'

'I can't help that.'

'You know, as Millennial Dawnists, we cannot condone divorce.'

'I'm not divorced. Just abandoned. And I'll remind you that Pastor Russell was also separated from his wife.'

'That's enough, Elaine. Leave theocracy to the men.'

Outside in the car park, the Pioneer stared at me across the asphalt. I felt his eyes bore through my clothes and into my heart. Perhaps he knew about the champagne. Then he hopped into his old BMW and drove away, making signs in the air as he went. I asked myself, why had life been so boring until I met Troy?

## 5.

Troy let me feel his muscles. He paid all our bills. We could hardly kick him out to go back to the bus shelters. He bought me fancy chocolates with liqueur in the middle. And he bought me knick-knacks from stalls at the Royal Easter Show and Luna Park. On the rides, we pressed together going round sharp corners. It's true I left school when I was young but then so did Pastor Russell, founder of the Witnesses.

When I asked Troy where he went at nights he replied, 'Out and about.'

When I asked him what he did when he went out and about he replied, 'A little of this, a little of that.'

I thought, I should be taking offence at this tone, I should slap him, like a modern girl. I worried that I was going out with an agent of Satan, because at the Last Judgment, we were told, the wicked will be annihilated and I would not like to see that.

'Why do you have to go out again?' I asked one night as he was getting ready. 'Don't you want to be with me?'

''Course I do, Shazza.'

'I don't want you to get annihilated.'

'I'll be careful.'

'That's not what I mean.'

'You know how much I love ya, Shaz. But your mum's driving me crazy. She's off her nut. She's always complaining about how buggered she is, but she works her ring off doing the vacuuming. She should learn to put her feet up.'

It was true. Mum was always cleaning the house in case the Pioneer or some of the other senior Witnesses of the

Company came for a Home Visit. I thought all mothers did that.

'You could help her,' I said.

Troy made a vomiting noise.

'You could cook.'

'I don't cook. I've got things to do.'

'What things?'

'Business.'

I loved it when Troy called me Shazza. It made me feel like a real person. But it was that word *business*—part of the triumvirate of evil I worried about.

## 6.

Troy asked Mum if he could borrow her car, the one he had paid off. Well, she could hardly say no. He didn't come back till three in the morning and woke me up by sliding naked into bed beside me. I didn't mind. It was like a Christmas present that was all my own.

## 7.

Mum said that if he wanted to borrow her car three or four nights a week, then the deal was he would have to come to the Company with us to hear the sermonettes. The car was, after all, registered in her name. Troy squirmed a bit, but after making a phone call, finally agreed. I was happy because if the Last Judgment suddenly struck he would not be annihilated and we could sit beside each other and let our thighs touch as the prayers kind of washed around us.

## 8.

There were strange phone calls in the middle of the night. Messages for Troy from someone who called himself Max, who said things like 'The proof of the pudding is in the tank.' And 'Fine feathers make fine feather dusters.'

I was to relay these messages exactly and not mix them up. In fact, the first time, he gripped my arm and made me recite the message exactly. I soon learned to race to the phone before Mum should take it into her head and answer it. Troy said I was a good message-taker.

## 9.

At the Kingdom Hall, the District Servants and Pioneers surrounded Troy, welcoming him into the Company. They asked all about his past and his conversion. When did he see the light? Troy held my hand, patting it like a fish, saying we were soon going to be married. That sentence made my innards go all soft and gooey. The District Servants, the Pioneers and other young men looked at each other and mumbled... You mean we weren't even married and yet we were cohabiting under the same roof? What would be next, fishing? Gambling? Abortion?

'It does not look seemly, Elaine, to have an unmarried man cohabiting under the same roof as your daughter,' said the Pioneer, paraphrasing something from the Book of Revelations.

Before Mum could get a word in, Troy wisecracked, 'Get off your hobby horse, mate, I'm going to make an honest woman of her. And what a woman!'

No one laughed.

'I hope you don't mean me, Troy,' said Mum. She giggled nervously.

'It's not like I'm asking her to have a blood transfusion, for Christ's sake,' said Troy.

I could see the looks of annihilation registering in their eyes. Several job offers were forthcoming from the men of the Company but Troy, he said he already had a job. 'Thanks all the same, chaps.' And if they needed any cheap electricals, then he was their man.

10.

One day, I came home from the blind and curtain shop where I worked as a receptionist and found Mum vacuuming the carpet like a whirling dervish. The furniture had been thrust aside all higgledy-piggledy, the new vacuum cleaner hot to the touch.

'Are we having a Home Visit?'

Her eyes looked pinned back in her head, her hair flung upwards as if she'd been riding a motorcycle.

'Hello, darling,' she said. 'No, we're not. I don't know about you, but I'm feeling really energised and alive today.'

'That's good.'

'I feel like I've been touched by the Spirit. All around me is white light.'

I unlocked the lock Troy had installed on our door. Troy was lying on the bed laughing his head off.

'She's vacuumed the same bit of carpet ten times.'

'What have you done?'

He kicked the cushions aside.

'I put some gas in her coffee.'

'What does that mean?'

'A bit of go-ey. Some gas. You know—amphetamines. You want some?'

I was horrified.

'You have to go and tell her.'

'Let's wait until she's finished.'

'No.'

'Go on.'

'No.'

I made him go and explain or I wouldn't sleep with him that night. Or maybe ever, I was that serious. I crept down the hall and listened at the door while he sat Mum down, gazing into her shrunken pupils and explained. It was quite complicated. When she twigged, Mum fell to her knees in shock and started praying loudly from Hebrews 11 and 12.

'Choosing rather to suffer affliction with the people of God, than to enjoy the pleasures of sin for a season.'

'It's all right, Elaine,' said Troy, calming her. 'It's okay. You feel all right, don't you?'

'I'm tainted,' she wailed.

Troy thought about this.

'But it's a nice feeling, isn't it? Taintedness. I haven't heard you humming like that in ages.'

Mum had to think about this.

'Yes... I suppose.'

'Then if you limit yourself to every three or four days, you'll be fine.'

'Fine?'

'You'll be tip-top. No worries.'

'I... yes... I... Can you get some more?'

'I'll get you the best.'

'I... I've never enjoyed myself so much.'

When eventually Troy came to bed, I said, 'That wasn't quite what I had in mind. I thought you'd be more... penitent.'

'I told you I'm not a Catholic.'

'I wonder what you really are, Troy Cole.'

'I'm the man of your dreams, babe. Get your gear off.'

## 11.

I guess that's where Mum's moral corruption began, unless you count all the gifts she received and accepted and her letting him sleep under our roof in the first place.

As I said, she wasn't a very good Witness. The bills got paid and we all had a great time in front of the plasma TV. Troy made us cocktails. But he was a bit erratic. Sometimes, if anything came on that he disapproved of, he would slam the TV off and send us to our rooms. It was kind of like he was running the house.

One week, I was so tired from working in the blind and curtain shop that I didn't go to The Kingdom Hall. Troy went instead. Later, he told me he received five job offers. The next day, three of the elders, all of them Pioneers, called around to the house to make sure I had not lapsed or drifted or whatever the phrase is. You couldn't drift very far, even if you wanted to, with them keeping tabs on everyone.

'I'm just tired, that's all,' I said.

'You want to be part of the 144, don't you, Sharon?'

'Of course I do.'

'Because if you lapse, we don't need to remind you, when Armageddon comes Jesus will simply cast you down with the rest.'

'I don't want to lapse.'

'Like a puff of smoke, the wicked shall cease to exist.'

'I'm not wicked.'

'In the Second Advent, for those who are wicked, death will mean total, absolute extinction. Do you know what that means?'

'I've got an idea.'

'Then we want you to commence Apologeticals next week.'

'Visiting? Who?'

'The Neighbourhood.'

'But what about the blind and curtain shop?'

'Sharon, we're not asking you.'

## 12.

So, while my mother was being corrupted, I was out early Saturday mornings delivering copies of the *Watch Tower* and *Awake!* to people who slammed doors in my face. They paired me with a pimply boy called Denzil who did all the talking. He never said a single sentence that didn't have the word Jesus in it somewhere. One hundred hours a month in religious service.

Meanwhile, Troy lay in bed while Mum whizzed about on the vacuum cleaner. He slept during the day while she went to her new job at the haberdashers and later borrowed her car to go out, doing this and that, here and there. He didn't even ask anymore. Just stamped about yelling, *Where are the bloody keys?* and going through her handbag.

One Saturday afternoon, I returned early from doorstep preaching and unlocked our door. He was asleep on the bed, naked, dead to the world. He'd said he didn't want to be disturbed and I could see what he meant. Underneath him, completely covering the bed was a thick blanket of cash. There must have been thousands. More. It was like a crust. He would not wake. There was a glass of water by the bedside, which I contemplated throwing over him, but Troy had warned me never to touch the water by his bed. He looked so peaceful, he didn't even stir when I slid a fifty out from under him to make up for my miserable morning with Denzil and Jesus.

13.

The money was tidied away in a bag at the bottom of the wardrobe. When I mentioned it, he said: 'I hope you didn't try to spend any because it's counterfeit and if you did try to spend it, that's a federal offence, which would make you an accessory after the fact. And if you told anyone else about it, I'd have to cut out your tongue.'

14.

When Mum missed the sermonette one week with all the vacuuming and haberdashery, the Pioneers came again to pester her.

She had run away once. They didn't want that to happen again. Once they get their hooks into you, these sects, they don't like to let go.

They said it would be a nice gesture if she were to host a communion service in our lounge room the following Saturday, the thirteenth of Nisan, eve of the eve of Passover. To welcome the light back into her life after her lapse.

'But I haven't lapsed,' she told them. 'I've been busy doing the housework.'

'Thousands now living will never die. Christ paid the supreme sacrifice as a ransom for the salvation of obedient witnesses. The prize of his life given for the 144,000 lucky souls. Don't you want to be part of that, Elaine, at one with Jesus ruling in Heaven? Don't you want to have a golden soul?'

'Yes. I do. So much.'

When they left, she had to run around throwing sheets over the TV and getting rid of all the whisky and wine bottles Troy had brought home. It made quite a stack.

## 15.

When the Company began to arrive for the Bible studies reading, parking all over the nature strip, Troy was still in the shower. I quickly had to lock the door, so they wouldn't see the tangled shemozzle in our room. Mum greeted them with a spread of bread and grape juice and ceremonial wine. I think she had already quaffed a few ceremonial wines to calm her nerves. We pushed the furniture back against the walls, like a siege. When the visiting Circuit Servants and Pioneers and their wives had all assembled, Denzil got the ball rolling with a report on how our Apologetical Visits had been progressing. Not well, unfortunately. Number of conversions: zero, although we had clocked up our hundred hours for the month. The visiting Circuit Servant commended him with: 'Ye are my witness, saith Jehovah, and I am God.'

Just then Troy came marching into the room wearing nothing but a towel around his waist, the tattoos hanging off him. You could have heard a pin drop.

'Oh,' he said. 'Hi.' Then, 'I forgot you lot were coming.'

Denzil looked flummoxed. The Pioneers all gave Troy an eyeful, and if you ask me he was a mighty eyeful to behold. Teeth like a flock of sheep and all that. Mum eventually came to the rescue.

'Ah Troy, there was a phone call for you earlier. Max, I think it was. He said to tell you, er, what was it again? Oh yes, *The pig is on the prowl.*'

'Max?' said Troy. 'Oh right. Max... Hmm... Pig on the prowl, eh? Thanks, Elaine. Shazza can I see you for a moment?'

He ducked out. I followed him down the hall.

'Listen, babe,' he said, over his shoulder, 'I gotta skedaddle for twenty minutes, then I promise I'll be back for the rest of your prayer meeting.'

'I don't want to stay here. Can I come with you?'

'Sorry, babe.'

He peeled off the towel as he reached the doorway of our room. Underpants everywhere. Man and wife? Not likely.

'Who *is* Max?'

'Max? Oh, Max isn't his real name.'

He threw on some clothes, slipped on his boots. Reefed out the bag with the money and squashed it into a backpack.

'They'll ask where you've gone,' I said.

'Make something up. Look, they're good for an alibi but this is a bit much, in a man's own lounge room. Jesus. See you in twenty, babe.'

He tried to give my cheek a peck but I turned my face away. I watched him sidle, that's the only word for it, out the back door and disappear. Then I walked back into the lounge room where the sermonette was really warming up— how after Jehovah's victory there would be no more poverty or war or old age or sickness or crime. Mum in a corner with a beatific smile on her face, rocking slightly. I took my place, pretending to listen. How measurements of the Great Egyptian Pyramids gave proof to predictions of the second coming of Christ's invisible return. How, after a thousand years of peace, Satan would be loosed upon the world for a last crack at seducing mankind. The Pioneer had a little froth at the corners of his lips. White light humming. We were just getting started on Isaiah 43, chanting under our breath, when there was an almighty crash at the front door.

# PING-PONG PRINCIPLE

The highlight of my week, sad to say, is the game of ping-pong I play with Lionel Hegarty. I am not sure if, by calling it ping-pong, I might be committing some political indiscretion. Lionel prefers to call it 'table tennis', which feels far too cosmopolitan for me. Ping-pong, table tennis—all this alliteration. We have a regular game, which I look forward to, to the detriment, frankly, of my other duties, which do not concern us here. I am hoping I shall be able to make a metaphor from this.

About Lionel: Lionel talks a lot. In fact, he never shuts up. This would be all right if what he said was not so inappropriate, so socially inept. He has a great, awkward knack, of which he is completely oblivious, of putting his foot in it. In short, Lionel hates lying. There is the nub of the matter. He never lies. When I first met him, he made a rather grandiose declaration that he was the sort of person who never lied. I did not believe him, of course. What sort of person never lies and then boasts about it? Lionel strives to tell the truth even in the face of dire unpopularity. He does this with a smile and a coy tilt of the head, as if he were starring in a butter commercial. There is something slightly galling about such relentless optimism. I dare not ask anymore how his weekends have gone, for fear of unleashing a torrent of endless enthusiasm. Life is always great. The weather sensational. The weekends have been fantastic. A further dread is that he may ask me about mine.

It is hard to deal with a person who never lies, whose weekends just get better and better. Once he told us of a fabulous party he had gone to in his twenties where, in accordance with the mood of the times, candles were lit. There was incense. Music. Atmosphere. Lionel described how he had leant over the table to pass the joint and the candle flame leapt up, setting his handspun alpaca wool jumper ablaze and rushing up his chest. He flapped his hands in recollection, patting out the remembered flames. Our supervisor, a straight-laced woman of sixty with affiliations to Scientology, listened to this story with an expression akin to the apperception of a bad smell. (We had been talking about dinner parties, catering, and so on.)

As I said, Lionel does not know when to shut up. You could see the supervisor file that bit of information away for later reference. I cannot see myself admitting to an employer that I had taken drugs in my youth, even if she asked. Lionel cannot see, in his quest for veracity, that it might be more discreet to pick and choose his moment, if not his audience. He cannot see that naked revelation is not an end in itself.

'Serve.'

I have surprised myself at the level of skill with which Lionel and I play our ping-pong. I did not know I had such reflexes. The pace is fierce and frenetic. It is no leisurely backyard swat; it is competitive and sweaty. Lionel keeps score.

He never cheats. I said before that it is the highlight of my week. This is not exactly so. To be perfectly honest it is the highlight of my day, so empty is it otherwise. We play every lunchtime after scoffing our sandwiches. On Mondays, after a weekend of not playing (of having a life), I am irritable and cranky. I put this down to a dearth of ping-pong, but there may well be other reasons that do not concern us here. Life.

Put that paddle in my hand.

'Serve.'

More about Lionel: Lionel is the IT guy. As such, given the tenets of his general attitudes and behaviour, I see him as somewhere or other along the autistic continuum. And this is in no way meant to be disparaging towards autistic people. This is the only way I can put up with Lionel's interminable cheeriness. I could accept such ebullience from a born-again Christian, but not from someone I have to work with every day. (Please don't ask me about my weekend.) Sisyphus had only the potential for happiness, not the guarantee. Perhaps I am what they call a grumpy bastard. Lionel is the type of fellow who cannot understand why other people do not, for example, cut their own hair. He has it down to a fine art. He saves himself ten dollars every time he does so, and this all adds up. He even cuts his wife's hair. Lionel is good at everything. He does not, for example, understand why I do not change the oil in my car myself. Think of the saving! He has offered to help me do this in his own garage, which is set up for just such purposes. There are other things he knows about that might save me money, which I cannot bear to think of at the moment.

Lionel jogs. Lionel cycles. Lionel kick-boxes. He says that the reason he has to stay trim is so his wife won't tire of him. I am not sure if I am meant to take this as a joke or not, so

I do. I laugh. That is the trouble with the truth, it can be so slippery and ambiguous. Lionel can do one hundred push-ups on his knuckles. Why can't everyone? Lionel is the go-to man if you want your computer fixed over the weekend when it starts not doing all those things you really need it to do. It is a great opportunity for him to explain what you are doing wrong. Of course, you take all this with a grain of salt because he is doing it for nothing.

About Lionel's wife: Trudy, herself equally trim and buffed, is just as optimistic about life in general, though the strain of living with Lionel is showing. Happiness surely cannot be so contagious. Once I saw her at a summer barbecue and her muscles were defined and brown as potatoes. I asked, in some amazement, if I could feel them and she said yes and they felt like steel and I told her so. Admittedly, I had had a few drinks by then. I am not normally the type who would ask to feel a strange woman's biceps but on that occasion it felt like the right thing to do and I was not rebuffed. Lionel tells me how he does everything for his wife. The cooking, the cleaning, the washing. He dotes on her. He's a liberated guy. Trudy, he says, is so kind and generous. She has a lot of projects. The house is paid off. Their kids are well-adjusted.

'Serve.'

I learn all this about Lionel's family while we are playing ping-pong. I learn, for instance, they have a friend who is having marital difficulties. Trudy feels sorry for him, Brad, the lost lamb whose wife has run off with a speedboat repair mechanic. Suddenly, in that moment, 19—18, I have lost track of who or what Lionel is talking about. Who is Brad? What are you talking about? What's the score? Is it not 18—19? There are too many characters in his life. I wish he would just serve the ball. When he talks to himself like this

I feel I have an ever so slight advantage; however, Lionel has a terrific backhand smash that I find intimidating and which more than makes up for his distraction.

Brad is Trudy's current project. (I'm lost again. Is he the speedboat mechanic?) She likes to include him in their family activities. Lionel gets on with Brad. They are modern blokes. They take him to the kids' soccer games. They take him to the Eagles Reunion Tour concert and sing 'Hotel California' together. They buy him clothes (or rather Trudy does, because Lionel has no fashion sense and would wear the same T-shirt until it fell off him, that's just the kind of guy he is). Listening, I think this arrangement does not sound quite tickety-boo. It sounds more like a recipe for disaster. However, it is something I do not really want to know anything more about when all I want him to do is serve.

We are evenly matched. Sometimes the contest is tight. Deuce, deuce, deuce. Sometimes he thrashes me. Sometimes I thrash him. When we play, there is no time to think. Once, he beat me thirteen games to zero. I barely made double figures. In thirteen games! I despair that I might never win another game of ping-pong again. I grieve that this is symptomatic of all else that seems to be going wrong in my life. I do not mention this to Lionel for fear of the advice he might offer. I tell myself, it's a confidence thing. In a spasm of shame it dawns on me that, because of my reticence, I have no one else that I can mention it to. It is probably a sad reflection on the emptiness of my own soul that I can expend so many words on the hitting of a little ball over a nylon net, although I acknowledge that plenty of souls before mine have probably been emptier.

One day, Lionel tells me, whether I want to hear this truth or not, that he has not had sex for over a year, he who has such a deep craving for physical affection.

'Serve.'

Each night, after he has washed the dishes and checked that the dog has enough water and the house is locked, he enters the marital bedroom to find Trudy feigning sleep on the far edge of the mattress. If he touches her, she groans and shrugs him off. So he has learnt to keep his distance across the no-man's land of the cold bed. It's a scene I can imagine with far too much alacrity.

He tells me, in comic exasperation, that Trudy has racked up a credit card debt of twenty-five thousand dollars, and he the only breadwinner. What do I think about that? I do not know what to say. I tell him it doesn't sound good. What does she buy? He doesn't know. Things for Brad—to cheer him up because he's so depressed. Lionel laughs at how ludicrous this sounds. I see now that Lionel is the sort of chap who giggles under pressure; that is, he deals with tension by smiling. There's a mixed message floating around here that I'm too depressed to untangle for him.

'Serve.'

I go through a winning patch. He cannot beat me. It's a confidence thing. Ace, ace, ace. My forehand smashes are unplayable. We analyse each game, where our strengths and weaknesses lie. It's like a dance. He tells me that, of the last eight nights, he has had only four hours sleep. What? He draws me a little equation: $0 + 0 + 2 + 0 + 1 + 0 + 1 + 0$. (The two being because he took a sedative and half a bottle of red.)

'Do you think that's healthy?' he asks. I say it doesn't sound good. How is it possible, he wonders, someone can survive on so little sleep? This raises the question, so I have to ask it: 'Why?'

He explains that, while servicing his numerous computers at home he has discovered some strange email traffic between his wife and (it isn't hard to find out) their friend Brad's computer. Investigating further, he finds there are dozens, if not hundreds. They are quite spicy. He tells me this as if I should be as surprised as he is; however, he does so in such a nonchalant, happy-go-lucky tone that it is hard to feel anything other than wryly amused. It's a joke, right? I make sympathetic noises. Mmm, mmm.

This is how his heart breaks, with a smile and a chuckle.

Because he is the IT guy, it does not take Lionel long to discover the photographs in the memory of her phone. Her pubic hair decorated with the seashells found on a recent excursion to the beach. It had been a lovely day. They'd had a picnic. He would recognise that pubic hair anywhere. Then the erotic movie Trudy has made of herself—herself and a hairbrush. Not the bristly end, he says, wanting me to get the complete picture. He is not sure if erotic is the right word; what word would I use? I'm the word guy. I say it sounds euphemistic, and he says exactly.

Do I want to see the movie, just to make sure? It's rather graphic.

There is a reluctant separation. There is talk of property division.

Fortunately, all this has no bearing on the ping-pong, other than putting Lionel off his game, which is to my momentary advantage. But I know he'll bounce back. The tide will turn. There is my metaphor. Resilience. Already he has started going out with one of our colleagues, who must feel sorry for him, although I should not presume her motives.

I saw Lionel sketching out an equation for her: $0 + 0 + 2 + 0 + 1 + 0 + 1 + 0$. From that it was easy to predict the outcome. She seems a nice girl, who looks remarkably like Trudy, but without the biceps. Far be it for me to pursue that comparison. This affair is skating along rapidly, so much so that I have to admire his quick work. Lionel is bouncing back. There is talk of their moving in together, of property amalgamation. I have to admire how adherence to the truth, something I am not very good at, or so I have been told, has given Lionel a particular way of being in the world—a moral principle, he has that at least, by which to live his life.

# THE ISTHMUS

Hector and I are on a touring holiday of the south. Since his retirement we have seen quite a lot of the country in our campervan, home away from home. Hector has a story for every place visited. He is a mine of information. Yesterday, we saw the bottomless, blue lakes of Mount Gambier and now we have arrived at the famed Twelve Apostles (although there are only eight), on Victoria's rugged south coast.

There, I might have written that on a postcard. Dear Grandchildren, the weather is a) sunny, b) overcast, c) wet, d) all of the above. Ah! must be in Victoria. Don't forget the date: Fifteenth of January, 1990. I would not write that; after all this time on the road, I am getting a bit fed up with Hector and his stories.

The Twelve Apostles, all eight of them, as you sweep around the coastal cliff top road are certainly a majestic sight, or is that a magisterial one? Hector parks the van and I buy a postcard from the stand in the kiosk. A touring coach has just disgorged its cargo of bus-sick passengers, half of them lined up outside the ladies toilet.

'Shall we have our picnic?' Hector asks.

'I should go to the lav first.'

'Look at that queue,' he says. 'Let's duck out over this London Bridge or whatever it's called, then have our sandwiches.'

'Yes, I'd kill for a cup of tea.'

Hector's Hawaiian shirt is a little garish for Victoria, so I ask him to put on his jacket.

The London Bridge is a spectacular limestone archway that leans over the water to a pair of conjoined, rocky outcrops. Although they are not technically Apostles, they do form a pretty distinctive feature of the cliffs and coastline. Actually, it is what they call an isthmus, with a couple of giant cavities burrowing through it like a Swiss cheese and the waves crashing through. I'll take a photo after lunch.

It feels nice to stretch our legs. It should only take a few minutes to wander out there and back and then a lovely cup of Liptons. So, we stroll across the road and down the gravel path and over the London Arch (its other name) and barely thirty seconds after we have crossed it, the ground behind us gives a shudder and a bark, and with a tremendous crash, collapses into the sea.

'Jesus,' says Hector, alarmingly. Hector never swears. Suddenly, he has his arm about my waist and is bustling me forward. Me, who has not bustled for years.

'Come on. Quick sticks.'

Behind us, or rather beneath us, the sea is boiling orange and white.

'What happened?' I ask, frightened.

'The bridge collapsed.'

It is an understatement but I might as well say it: 'Lucky we weren't still standing on it.'

'Yes Caroline, that's the understatement of the year… Jesus.'

'No need to swear.'

Both of us are trembling with the close shave of it, staring stupidly at the water below. I can smell fresh rock.

'We're trapped.'

Even I can see how obvious that is. We are now suddenly alone on what is evidently a newly created limestone pillar. An island, albeit a small one. We can still hear bits of the pinnacle, great slabs of rock carving off and falling into the sea. Hector nudges me to what he estimates is the geometrical centre of the island. It is only a matter of about twenty paces in any direction to the edge. It is so narrow I could throw a stone from one side to the other. And I'm not much of a shot. I can barely throw a ball of rolled up socks across the lounge room. Oh, I could if I was angry enough, but Hector hasn't done enough to annoy me yet. Give him his due.

There is another, second archway linking our pinnacle to a smaller one further out to sea, but there is no way I am going to cross that. Hector is right; we are trapped. Exiled. Forty metres up in the air on a teetering limestone tower. Actually, it is only the clouds scudding by that give the impression the limestone is teetering.

Over on the opposite cliff, people are calling, waving. I can see tourist buses and our own little van in the car park. People stand back from the edge because I guess their side of the cliff is still crumbling, too. They wave to us. We wave back. The welcome humanity of it. No man is an island and no woman either, I suppose. There is a slight breeze from the south; on a warm day, this could possibly be described as being as refreshing as the beads of condensation on a cold glass of chardonnay. Only, it's not a warm day. It appears no one knows what to do, neither the people on the mainland, nor us. We can make out the windswept squeak of their voices, but not what they are shouting. The isthmus is gone. We are stuck.

Gradually, it comes to me that I still need to go to the toilet.

'Looks like we might be here for a while, old girl.'

'Don't call me old girl.'

'May as well pull up a pew.'

Hector sits, grunting, on the bare ground. I sit beside him, watching the figures on the far cliff watching us. There is nothing else to do.

'Wish we'd brought the picnic basket,' he says after a while.

'Hmph.'

'Pincher Martin ate seaweed on his rock. I guess we could eat—what is this stuff?—moss?'

'You can eat moss. I'm sitting here till we're rescued.'

I can be stubborn when I want to be. No one seems to be doing anything. More buses arrive on the far escarpment. There seems to be lots of excitement over there. I guess we can already divide our ordeal, in the manner of the marooned, into the time before we sat down and the time after we sat down. It is, in my experience, an unprecedented situation.

It's strange how ideas come into Hector's head, because out of the blue he says, 'I wonder if this means there are now nine Apostles?'

'Oh shut up, Hector. I'm cold.'

'Do you want my jacket?'

'And have you catch your death again!'

There is a modicum of warmth where our shoulders touch. Uncharacteristically, he puts his arm around me and gently squeezes.

'Buck up, old duck.'

'Don't call me old duck.'

'Do you know these limestone stacks were formed during the Neogene period between five and twenty-three million years ago?'

'How do you know that?'

'I read a brochure last night.'

'Well, that's not going to help us get off it.'

'The cliffs and stone stacks erode two centimetres a year. That figure must be an average because that bit,' he waves his arm, 'just eroded about two hundred metres in one go.'

'That's not reassuring.'

'No.'

He glances around to make sure we are quite in the middle.

'Hector?'

'Yes, Caroline.'

'I need to go to the loo.'

'You should have gone before we came across.'

'You saw that queue. You were the one who said we'd just nip over and back.'

'Don't get snappy with me. I didn't know the blasted bridge was going to collapse.'

'Neither did I.'

Silence for a while. He looks east. I look west. A seagull lands on our island and glares at us as if to say, *Where are your sandwiches?* A part of me wonders, in the manner of the marooned, if only I were a seagull, but I am aware there is no profit to be had from this train of thought.

I shift uncomfortably on my bottom.

'Try to take your mind off it,' says Hector.

'All right for you to say.'

'Do you realise we are the first people ever to set foot on this island.'

'And the last. No one in their right mind would shimmy up forty-metre cliffs to say, *Ooh, look, there's nothing here*.'

'I'm trying to be helpful, Caroline.'

'Well, you're not.'

Pause.

'Shall we play *I Spy*?'

'Shut up.'

'Don't you have a postcard? We could fill that in.'

'I don't have a pen.'

'Just like Pincher Martin, ha ha.'

We watch the clouds for a while. One could get too used to that.

'Do you know that the Twelve Apostles used to be called the Sow and the Piglets?'

'Why did they change it?'

'Not grand enough. I don't know. Why do they change anything?'

I am beginning to wonder what might happen if we have to spend the night here. That thought is too awful to contemplate. Surely someone on the mainland is telephoning for assistance.

'I guess we have naming rights,' I say. 'What shall we call it, our island?'

'That's the girl. Let's put on our thinking caps.'

The sweet, chardonnay breeze at our backs has turned into an Antarctic gale. It's freezing, all the way from the South Pole. Perhaps the Twelve (nine) Apostles are icebergs that looked back at Lot's wife.

'Thinking caps will blow off in this hurricane,' I say.

'What about—The Windy Isle?'

'The Island of Hector Moreau.'

'Nice,' says Hector. 'The Sandwichless Island.'

'Island With No Trees. Or toilets.'

'Or banks. Or anything. We can create civilisation anew.'

'I was perfectly happy with civilisation the way it was, and then you had to drag me off in a silly campervan.'

Hector is not listening. He is getting into the swing of things. He waves his arm grandly about the new, treeless island.

'King and Queen of all they survey.'

'Shut up, Hector… I don't think I can hold on much longer.'

'Steady on, old girl. I think some of those people over there have telephoto lenses. We'll be on the front page of the local rag for sure.'

Hector is laughing at me. His shoulders are quietly shaking. We could not be more estranged if we were on a desert isle in the middle of the Pacific with a lone palm tree between us. I wonder if I could push him off the edge and blame it on the wind, but there appear to be too many witnesses with telephoto lenses.

'What am I going to do? I'll get cystitis if I hang on any longer.'

The sound of the waves far below is an agony.

'You'll just have to hide behind me.'

'Oh, my Gawd.'

There is nothing else for it. I slowly ease my way behind Hector so we are sitting, well—squatting, back to back. I would give a lot for a palm tree right now. Hector is a slight man so there is not a lot of him to hide behind. He spreads wide the wings of his jacket like a cormorant. I make adjustments to my dress and nether garments and the relief is immediate and profound.

Hector calls out: 'Island of Pissing in the Wind.'

I jab my elbow backwards and make satisfying contact with his kidneys.

'Ouch.'

The edge is just there. So easy. The blue lake, yesterday, had been tempting.

At that moment, we hear the chest thumping whap whap whap of a helicopter approaching from the Peterborough direction.

'Better hurry up, old girl. Here comes the cavalry.'

'I am hurrying.'

I pray, please don't let them have a TV crew. I smooth my dress down. Hector folds his wings. I guess the Antarctic gale is not quite as windy as I thought because the helicopter, with a sightseeing logo painted on the side, descends towards us. We have to shuffle away from the centre of the island to give it room. This is terrifying because the cliffs seem much steeper than they did when I first looked at them. Precipitous, I think is the word.

The helicopter does dance about in the wind a bit, but finally it touches down on the mossy rock. A search and rescue fellow, or maybe it is a fireman, jumps out and beckons us towards him. The tornado from the rotor blades plays havoc with my dress and my hair. I fear it will get caught in the propeller thingy and have me off, like a loaded Hills Hoist in a cyclone. It is a fair jump from the mossy rock up to the helicopter. I hang in the doorway. Hector and the fireman each get a shoulder underneath my ballast and heave. I tumble, head first up and into the chopper, sprawling all over the floor. Then Hector is there beside me, clinging to my arm and the pilot turns to us with a grin and a thumbs up.

It is hard to believe how short that helicopter flight is. How short and how joyless. I wonder if I could tip Hector out the open door, blaming the blustery conditions, but he already has a seat belt on. In a very brief interlude he learns that the reason the pilot took so long was that he was out surfing. My hair has barely settled by the time we touch down on the other side. The mainland. Civilisation. I am still deeply flushed at the indignity of my rescue. There is an ambulance and the fellow gives us both the once over. They place blankets about our shoulders and ask a few questions but there is not much to say, really, about being stuck on a limestone rock for a few hours with nothing on it but a seagull. Hector makes a joke about returning from exile, about eating moss. People are more interested in photographing the collapsed bridge. That is, its absence. Pretty soon they let us go, and I am more than happy to fade into the general background of the afternoon where the idea of the front page is nothing but a bad dream.

We wander, light-headedly, over to the campervan. When the doors close, the snug fit encloses us like an embrace. It is very quiet. The wind muffled. We both breathe softly together. Another tourist coach arrives and spews out a load of happy photographers. The sea has returned to its normal colour. The approaching dusk is painting the Twelve Apostles a rusty orange. Endless rhythm of the waves.

'Only a little hurt pride, eh, Caroline?'

'Only.'

'Something to tell the grandkids.'

I grunt. The isthmus between us. I am sure my hair must look a fright. Eventually, Hector reaches into the back of the van and hoists the picnic basket onto his lap. He opens it. He hands me a tin mug. He pours. The tea is still warm.

'Thermos Island,' he says, and it's just the two of us once more.

# BRIDIE

By 9:30 most weeknights, Dean hoped to be warmly ensconced in his bed. Most nights he was. Dean was not the spring chicken he used to be. A sweet dream was forming in the depths of his grey matter, when it was rudely interrupted (at 11:03!) by a tentative knock, like the tapping of the dog's tail on the floor. Dean stumbled from the bedroom, knotting the cord in his pyjamas. The conscious, but slightly frazzled part of his mind knew he should look through the peep hole or at least call out but he didn't. Home invaders wouldn't knock so timidly, would they? He pulled the door open to the night's cold lung and there, beneath his line of vision, stood Bridie.

Bridie was the kid from down the road. She was younger than Dean's daughter Grace (who was at that moment fast asleep) and was known in the neighbourhood as something of a feral child. Words to that effect. Her hair unbrushed and awry, she was dressed only in her school tunic.

'I've been waiting at home,' she began, 'and my mum hasn't come back yet.'

Dean blinked. He did not immediately have a response to this information. What mum? He was in two minds about Bridie. The sort of kid who always had scabbed knees and liked to play in gutters. Dean remembered that once she'd brought her pet albino rat to show Grace, only she had dropped it on the floor and a bit of its tail had fallen off.

'You'd better come in,' Dean said, who had once enjoyed playing in gutters, picking his scabs—all a long time ago. Bridie entered. Everyone else was asleep.

'Aren't you cold, Bridie?'

'No, I never get cold.'

'When is your mum coming back?'

'In about an hour.'

Bridie looked around and Dean tried not to wonder if she might be casing the joint.

'Right. So you've spoken to her?'

'No.'

'She left you a message?'

'Deano, who is it?' Shona's sleepy voice mumbled from the bedroom. He secretly hated her calling him Deano. Dean went to her, bundled beneath the blankets. The light bulb set Shona squinting.

'It's Bridie. Her mum's not home.'

'I'll make up a bed for her.'

Shona did not move, other than to raise her head a little.

'No. It's all right, she's coming back. I'll go and wait with her.'

'Good. Thanks, Deano.'

Shona let her head fall back on the pillow. Dean contemplated leaving the light on. His secret hates were starting to outnumber his public ones.

Outside, the night was freezing. Fog huffed from their mouths as if they were smoking. The dog did not want to come with them. After a few steps, Dean began to feel decidedly uncomfortable being outside at this time of night in his dressing gown. Wind whipped at his ankles, making his pyjama pants flap like flags. In the trees possums worried him.

'Are you sure you're not cold, Bridie? I am.'

'I never get cold.'

The kid was perfectly calm and self-contained. She strolled along at his side. Dean told her that she had done the right thing coming to get help instead of sitting at home by herself.

She agreed.

'When did you last see your mum?'

'This morning.'

'How do you know she'll be back in an hour?'

'She always comes back.'

He recalled seeing the mother with her dreadlocks walking into town. She never drove. No, it could not rightly be called walking; Dean thought the term must be trucking. Perhaps wandering was best, aimlessly or purposefully, it didn't matter, Dean identified with it. Yet, he freely admitted, he didn't know the woman from a bar of soap.

Bridie lived six or seven houses down the street, but there were no other local kids, so it was natural that she should have picked out Grace's house—the animal magnetism of kids. Good fences, good neighbours. Her house was wide open with every light ablaze. The TV deafening. Dean wanted to call out, but in the end just followed her in. Screen door a-clatter behind him. The late news repeated grisly footage of the latest war. Dean would never have let his daughter sit up and watch the war footage, especially so late at night. The house looked like a bomb had hit it. His first thought was that perhaps it had been burgled, then he realised that it was nothing more than an ordinary, domestic mess. The sort of mess he recognised as dormant in himself and had, over the years, successfully repressed. Yes. He certainly did not want to judge anyone else, touch wood, on the strength of their messes.

'Have you had any dinner?' He yawned.

'I et some chips.'

They wandered about the house. He was trying not to pry, but now that he was here, by gum he may as well be curious. He wasn't quite sure what he was looking for that would render his own life so uninteresting by comparison. A part of him, the histrionic part, even wondered if the mother might be dead in a bedroom. But no, no, no. The sink was full of filthy dishes. The air smelled of stale smoke. He spied old roaches in an ash tray, crumbs of dope on the table top, empty chip packets scattered about the television. Those were the days. The calendar on the fridge had not a day circled on it. This was as close to anarchy as he could imagine.

'So you've been waiting here by yourself since you got home from school?'

'Yep.'

'Where's she gone, your mum?'

'Out to a party. She works very hard and needs to take time out to relax.'

'Did she tell you to say that?' (May as well be presumptuous, he thought, I'm the adult here.)

'No. It's true.'

'Does your mum have a phone?'

'She didn't pay the bill.'

'Hmm... so you don't exactly know if she'll be home in an hour or not.'

'I think she will. She always comes home.'

On the news the body count was updated. Pie charts and bar graphs described the state of the conflict. Dean knew they couldn't stay here. Imagine if the mother came back to find a strange man in his pyjamas in her house with her daughter. Besides, he was now witness to her, not to put too fine a point on it, evident squalor. Where would he sit? It was Shona who had met the mother, offered her a lift once or twice, had commented on her dreadlocks. In his heart, Dean had nothing whatsoever against dreadlocks.

'What happened to your pet rat?' he asked.

'It ran under the couch and all the other rats that live there killed it.'

Dean looked at the couch. It had an aura, he thought, of many things. He moved away from it. Apart from some newspapers, it was strewn with clothes, clean or dirty he could not tell. Did they move? An open packet of ear-buds lay spilled on the floor. The shade about the light was full of dried moths. He made a sudden, executive decision to return to his own home with Bridie and make up a bed for her on the lounge. (Trust Shona to be right about that, too.)

He left a note on the kitchen bench, first clearing a corner so the note would not be lost in the general clutter. He wrote his phone number, then scribbled it out, remembering that Bridie's phone had been cut off. Then he considered that the mother (he didn't even know her name!) might think he did not want her to contact him, so he wrote another note, this time leaving his phone number intact. He was trying to do the right thing here. It was the bloody mother who was off gallivanting about town, after all. He did not turn off the lights.

After thinking about it for a few steps, Dean went back and retrieved the note, pinning it eventually to the outside of the door where it couldn't be missed. Street lights glowed wanly through the fog. The last train hooted. It was a forlorn sound he never grew tired of. One or two darkened dogs a-yap behind fences. Their paws scratching the gravel. The sound of possums. Back at Dean's house, Bridie said she was hungry. Dean yawned. The kid didn't look sleepy at all. He made her some cheese and pickles on toast, which she proceeded to wolf down. He was now so tired himself that he wondered if he should just go to bed and let her have the run of the place; but all he really knew of Bridie was that she was supposedly feral. Something to that effect. Some gossip. Trust did not come into it. Seemed rather placid, really, kinda sweet, if that word was allowed anymore. Grace hadn't wanted to play with her much since the business of the rat. They had a shared interest in puddles, but that was as far as it went. Grace said Bridie was a little bit weird.

* * *

They were sitting on the floor playing dominoes. The only sound was the soft click of the tiles. It was after two o'clock. Dean wondered if he should take tomorrow—no, it was now today—off but what sort of excuse was that, to sit up with a feral kid till her mum came home? Why didn't she just go to sleep? Dean's jaw stretched as he yawned again.

Eventually there was a knock at the door. Not even the dog moved.

'Who is it?'

'Father Christmas,' a voice growled.

Father Christmas? What the—? I don't have time for these—Dean was angry. He threw open the door. A man stepped into the light. He was wearing a leather jacket. Dean took a step backwards at the sight of it.

'Who the—?'

A map suddenly appeared in his mind, on it were the locations of the nearest blunt instruments. The knives. Just in case.

'Where's Bridie?' said the man through an odour of alcohol.

For a moment Dean lost it. 'Who the fuck are you?'

'Where's the kid?'

'I beg your pardon?'

Glancing at Dean's pyjamas, the man's aggression abated with a hiss.

'Sorry... Shit... Look, sorry mate. It's been a shit of a night. All there is is this note saying you've taken the kid.'

'That's right. She's here.'

'Well, I've come to fetch her home.'

'Well, I repeat. Who the fuck are you?'

Dean had had time to analyse his feelings about the leather jacket and had decided that it was only a leather jacket after all.

'I'm Paul.'

'Well piss off, Paul...Where's the mother?'

'Mate, look, we've been at the pub, she's drunk as a skunk. Too embarrassed to show her face.'

Paul was now trying as best he could to relay some of this embarrassment. From the far end of the room Bridie called, 'Is that Mum?'

'It's a man called Paul,' said Dean. 'Do you know him?'

'Hi, Paul,' she called again.

Paul poked his head around the door and smiled at Bridie. The girl picked herself up and walked past Dean out into the night as if the whole thing had been neatly arranged. Parental pick-up after handy child minding. Thanks so much. Owe you one. Toodles. Dean was not sure if he should let the child go, but he could hardly snatch at her.

'Bridie, do you know this man?'

'He's Paul.'

'Mate,' said Paul, 'it's cool. I'm the boyfriend. Look, we're sorry about the hassle. Her mum's too upset. Domestics. We thought it was a kidnap. She asked me to come. I'll get her to come around tomorrow to explain. Thanks for looking after her.'

After this speech, Dean watched them climb the steps and fade into the shadows. The street lights looked odd at this time of night. Then he went to bed. His side of the mattress was stone cold.

In the morning he felt as though the—what was it?—incident—had not happened at all. He was only reminded of it when Grace asked over breakfast, 'Have you been playing with my dominoes again?'

When he packed them away he found one of the tiles was missing.

* * *

The mother did not come around to explain anything. In fact, Dean suspected that apart from some general, abstract humiliation, she had no recollection of her part in the evening either. Those were the days. Shona seemed to have no idea what had occurred during the previous night, snoring away in her bliss, only that Deano was in a grumpy mood again. He felt this was an unjust imputation and stewed quietly in his resentment. There was a certain tension about breakfast. Then he saw that he should not, as he would otherwise normally be accused of, be thinking solely about himself. So he thought about Bridie. The poor brat had probably been left on her own more times than she'd had hot dinners and who had sat up with her? Me, me, me. He wondered, is this the sort of case he should report to DOCS, or whatever the bloody authorities called themselves? Child negligence? God forbid Dean should be a witness to anything. And that bloke Paul certainly didn't fill him with confidence. And what would he tell them? That he wandered about the moonlit streets in his pyjamas with the girl shivering at his side?

No, not shivering, she'd said she wasn't cold…

Hmm.

A likely story.

* * *

The first Dean knew of it, Grace had informed him that Bridie, whom she'd never got on with anyway, was moving. Moving? How could such people afford to pack up and move? He knew the answer to that one. How quickly desperation could drive you.

They were having a garage sale. Getting rid of some of their stuff.

After some interrogation, Grace admitted she had never heard Bridie speak of a man called Paul, but then the only thing they'd ever had in common was an interest in puddles. They weren't friends. Didn't he understand that?

So, leashing the dog, wrapping themselves in coats, they took a walk, he and Shona. A nice, sunny afternoon. This could well be the end of everything, he thought. Who cared anymore about desperation? It seemed almost a normal state of being. Shona restrained the dog with both hands. All the furniture at Bridie's house was lumped higgledy-piggledy over the side of the road, down the driveway, leaning into bushes. There wasn't a great deal. Dean wondered if maybe this fellow Paul had gone berserk and thrown everything out onto the road. But no—there was Bridie, amidst boxes, behind a sign proclaiming *4 Sal*. Grace dawdled on, following a drain, as was her right.

'Hello, Bridie,' Dean said, 'are you moving?'

'Yep,' said Bridie, looking at her shoe.

'How is your mum?'

'She's asleep.'

'Is she well?'

'Yep.'

Not meeting his eye. Surrounded by her things. *4 Sal*.

'Did you get home safely the other night?'

'Yep.'

'Do you know what happened?'

'She came home. I told you, she always comes home. I go to school. Same as before. Now we're moving.'

'What about that fellow, Paul, the boyfriend?'

'He's not her friend anymore.'

'Did he do this?' Waving his hand at the furniture.

'No. He's a lazy cunt.'

'Who helped you move all this stuff out here?'

'Me mum. Who else? The truck'll be here soon.'

'Well, I hope it doesn't rain.'

'Me too… Hey Mister, how much will you give me for this couch?'

Dean moved on and did not reply. The trees overhead shushed in the strengthening breeze; it was always windy this time of year. Currawongs tuned their pipes in the elastic branches. Grace and Shona and the dog dawdled ahead. He felt appalled that he did not want to catch them up. If the wind were to drop it might be cold enough to snow. Every footstep felt the same.

# STEALTH

During the filming of the climactic scene in the action-packed Hollywood blockbuster *Stealth*, I was chief fire officer for the Megalong Valley CFA. I have not seen the film myself, not being much of a movie-goer, but I am told it is close to a masterpiece. Or maybe that is a masterpiece of extravagance? Either way, it reflects well, even though only a few minutes of my work made it into the final film. A few minutes, after all that effort, with Ross Livingstone losing his work shed, and kissing goodbye to an old Harley-Davidson he was working on in pieces on the floor. All up in smoke. Ah well! Sad but true. My son, Barry, wants me to take him to see the film, but I don't think it's an appropriate sort of entertainment, what with all the violence and 'adult themes'.

It's a long story. But in a nutshell, *Stealth* is a tale about an intelligent jet-fighter plane that wants to save the free world by blowing the billy-o out of the hanging swamp along Mount Hay Road. I don't know what the free world has to fear from the hanging swamp along Mount Hay Road. The producers claimed that blowing the billy-o out of things was in keeping with the plane's character and therefore crucial to the plot. You don't really expect Hollywood producers to come up with sensible explanations. It makes you wonder where they cook up these ideas. The hanging swamp was supposed to represent a desert of some kind, the kind of desert that harboured evil terrorists. Unfortunately, the swamp was also home to some endangered skink, or butterfly or rare parasite that lives only in the roots of the moss that grows there. Not sure if I've got the right end of the stick here. When we read this in the *Gazette*, Barry said he didn't want the butterflies to be blown up. He likes butterflies. And skinks. And birds.

This is where the greenies stepped in, taking the law into their own hands. 'Save the parasites,' they shouted. They chained themselves to gates; lay down in the path of the napalm; chanted, *We shall not be moved*, even though there were only about twenty of them. After a few photographs, the police dragged them off.

It worked. Unfortunate for Hollywood, but lucky for us, the protesters won. A victory for the environment; a victory for the defenceless. As you'd expect, being a big budget block-buster, money was no object. The *Stealth* producers shopped around. They offered Ross Livingstone (after he rang up and volunteered) a bucketful of dosh to let them transfer the location of the shoot (I've got all the lingo) from the hanging swamp up on the mountain, down into the shadows of the valley where they could blow the billy-o out of his property, on which he ran several horses and a few head of shivering cattle. Think of the money these Yanks would bring down into the valley, Livingstone argued in the community hall. They would need accommodation. And they would need dinner. And breakfast. And probably lunch. They would eat the teashop out of house and home. It would be an economic boom.

So we agreed. The valley is a magical place, as anyone will tell you. The cliffs of Narrowneck plateau rise to the east, so that each day begins like a kid poking his face up over a fence. Barry, who has an affinity with animals, would ride a horse from sunup to sunset if he could, all the way over the Cox to the Wild Dogs and back. And the horse would do that for him. But as Ross said, money is money.

Even though the location had changed, the valley was still meant to represent the desert. The intelligent fighter plane, Stealth, was supposed to be able to fly through the night sky like a bat, reading people's thoughts and such-like but I don't reckon the producers rated the intelligence of the audience too highly. Continuity, I think it's called. Or lack of it. Since when did the Megalong Valley look like a desert?

Anyhow, they splashed their big bucks around, sneered at the greenies, and Ross Livingstone said, yes, they could blow up whatever they wanted on his property. Within reason. They couldn't touch his shed, for example. He'd need some guarantee. That's where the Country Fire Authority came in. The biggest controlled explosion in the, oh I don't know, the Southern Hemisphere? Something like that. It was certainly bigger than the last cracker night we had down in the valley before they were banned. And much cheaper for them, blowing up things here in Australia than in their own back-yard. I examined their permit and it was all above board. So, fire away. I thought Barry might get a good memory out of all the razzle-dazzle.

Our job was to help plant the pyrotechnics. That is, to supervise the Hollywood powder monkey while he wired up the Nitropril and detonators, poured petrol—petrol by the tanker load—down the trunks of hollow trees, into rabbit burrows, all over Livingstone's doomed but profitable property. They were very professional. Only once, in my official capacity, did I have to tell them that they were pouring their diesel in a trench too close to the creek that fed the Cox, which was part of the Sydney water catchment and might get a few people jumping up and down. It was a disaster waiting to happen. They were pretty good about it. They didn't want another environmental fuss on their hands.

But Ross told me to keep my damn nose out of it. It was his private property, he said, and he had given permission to blow up anything the director thought would look good cart-wheeling through the air on fire. So long as they paid. It was a deal they had and he didn't want me to put the mockers on it. The director said he did not wish to enter into local politics, he was simply remaining faithful to the script; this project had artistic integrity. And money was no object in the pursuit of artistic integrity. I couldn't help thinking that he was making it up as he went along. There was talk of shooting a scene where the intelligent fighter plane confronted the greenies about the value of parasites and the value of life in general, thereby developing his character to a more sophisticated level, but underneath realising that the greenies were really terrorists and didn't care a hoot about the value of life, no, they only cared about power and so deserved to have the billy-o blown out of them. I don't know if that scene made it into the final film.

It was all very interesting how they went about things. My second-in-command, Barry, jiggled from foot to foot in anticipation. He was hoping to meet movie stars. He was eighteen and this sure made a change from the quiet life in the shadows he was used to. A dead kangaroo on the side of the road is about as much excitement as we get around here and takes a bit of working through. He watched them set up their caravans and catering tents and camera dollies and all the other film paraphernalia. But the only stars in this scene were a handful of extras and stuntmen who were to play corpses in the desert. Even Stealth, the star of the show, was back in a studio hangar somewhere.

Once they were all set up, Mrs Lewis brought over some scones and homemade jam from the teashop, but the crew only wanted their hotdogs and Pepsi. Did they not want anything at all from the local shop? No thanks, Ma'am, they were fully self-sufficient. Barry and I loved her scones so we tucked in. Barry asked a stuntman for his autograph. And got it. He clutched the piece of paper like a jewel, showed it to Mrs Lewis.

'That's lovely, Barry.'

Any road, it took ages to prepare the location. Barry followed the powder monkey around getting in everyone's way. You might have thought he was taking lessons although, God knows, lessons were wasted on him. Eventually, they were ready. All they had to do was wait for nightfall. The mobile phones rang hot, synchronising watches and so forth. Dusk came and went, turning the cliffs of the escarpment all around us orange. The faces in the sandstone were changing with the light. It was a clear evening. Roos abounded. No wind. I thought the cliffs would have looked real beaut in a film if you were making a film about cliffs, but I guess they didn't look much like the desert either. Barry gazed at them in rapture.

'Barry,' I called, 'put your jumper on. It's getting cold.'

He didn't hear me. I had to take the cotton wool out of his ears and repeat myself.

'Birds,' he said, pointing to the sky.

Eventually the director called—*Lights! Camera! Action!* No. No lights. It was nighttime. Just action, then. In the distance, coming from Medlow, a little Cessna flew overhead with a few red lights blinking. This was simply for the cameras and the bad guys on the ground to track through the sky. Continuity again. They think of everything. Later they would get a computer to superimpose Stealth stealthily traversing the treacherous terrain, pinpointing the location of the bad guys with his infrared, X-ray vision. Funny really, because according to the plot, Stealth was supposed to be able to read people's thoughts and empathise with their predicaments and be a protagonist for good, before offering helpful advice in the cause of peace and ultimately blowing the billy-o out of them. Oh well.

Livingstone, standing alone on his porch, watched all this activity with interest.

Then came the wanton destruction. *Ka Boom!* as they say in the comics. The ground trembled and bucked, which made Barry widdle. I gasped to my boots. Flames reached the moon, or so it seemed from our point of view. Whole trees exploded into kindling. The escarpment glowed ochre and shimmered. They had cameras all over the place to capture every flaming, spinning piece of debris, moment by moment. Parallel lanes of flame burst through the night. Pity the poor parasites, not to mention all the other wildlife about the place, blown to smithereens. The noise of it was truly deafening. Echoes rumbled to every corner of the valley. Some of the extras lay dead on the ground. Burning birds flew like comets. The bonnet of one of Livingstone's old Bedford trucks erupted high into the air and floated down like a piece of flaming pastry. It was like the ending of the world. Very speccy.

Then came our turn. Once all the pyrotechnics had blown off and the director had yelled *Cut*, through his loudspeaker, or *That's a wrap*, or whatever he said, my team of volunteer fireys ran around with their extinguishers and hoses dousing the flames where they were beginning to spread. A blaze down in Livingstone's gully almost got away into the bush, but luckily the tanker was down that way with the new pump paid for by a sausage sizzle and meat tray raffle. It worked a treat and a real disaster was averted. Good work, lads.

I don't suppose even Hollywood can plan for every contingency. Unfortunately, the Bedford bonnet, flaming down from orbit, crashed through the roof of Livingstone's shed and set the whole shop on fire. Oil and grease everywhere, it's no surprise. It was lit up like a Christmas tree by the time anyone noticed. That is, a Christmas tree doused in oil and grease and set ablaze. Ross ran around shouting but I don't think they got any footage. In about three minutes, the shed was a pile of smoking rubble. Where was my crew? Nowhere to be seen. Eventually, I found Barry around the back, his face turned up to the stars, fireman's helmet hanging from his chin by its strap, his jaw agape. I could still see the dancing sky aflame in his eyes. He did not hear me until I pulled the plugs from his ears.

'It's all over now, son.'

He looked at me, putting the words together.

'Dad, can we do that film again?'

As the evening began to wrap up, Livingstone complained loudly about the shed, but Hollywood thought they had paid him more than enough. They had all the footage they wanted. He could buy a new shed. All this while they were bumping out. The situation was what the Americans called a YP not an OP. That is, it was Your Problem not Our Problem. So then, he complained loudly that the CFA had not done their job properly and we ought to compensate him for the loss of his antique Harley-Davidson which had been inside the shed and was now underneath the smoking rubble. When no one showed any interest, he complained loudly about the sort of people the CFA had working for them. Cretins. Look at them. Some of them couldn't even tie their own shoelaces. I told him that if he spoke about my son like that again, I'd drop him on his arse as soon as look at him. He did not respond, other than with the closure of his jaw. The film crew then stowed their cameras, tents and other gear into the vans and drove in convoy back up to the swishy Hydro Majestic hotel on the cliff top, leaving us to mop up any spot fires, although after Livingstone's tirade no one was very enthusiastic. We all wanted to go home to bed.

The next morning, not too early, Barry and I were back, wandering through the carnage of the landscape. Tendrils of smoke drifted in the air. It was like a bomb—well, yes, I suppose a bomb had hit it. It was surreal, like—well, yes, like being in a movie. I'm not saying this right. Barry was horrified; charred and blackened patches of earth, trees uprooted and flung aside, fences ruined, charcoal scars, the bush scorched to ash. On neighbouring properties, horses and sheep trembled up against the most distant gates. Cows did not come in for milking. It looked—well, yes, like a war zone, which I guess was what the producers were after. Veris-(I looked this up)-imilitude. It was very lifelike. The sad bit was—all that aftermath and not a camera in sight.

While Livingstone was busy mourning the loss of his shed and composing letters of complaint, Barry found a splintered, devastated tree, laid flat like a twisted civilian. In the soft light of day, it was hard to see how Livingstone's bottom paddock could even remotely resemble a desert filled with terrorists. More full of nervous kangaroos with the squitters than terrorists. A giant angophora had been felled by one of the blasts. Barry walked its length. I followed slowly, extinguishing coals and hot spots underneath with a burst of foam. I watched him peel a strip of torn bark from the trunk. Angophora sap is red, so it looked like he was peeling back flesh from a human wound. Under the bark was a small hollow where a dozen little bats huddled together in the smoke and steam. They shifted their wings as if shielding their faces from the light. Barry made some soft noises and nudged them with his finger. As we watched they flapped their leathery wings and rose together in a spiral, like stars around a cartoon character's head. Barry watched them, willing them upwards, his neck craned back.

The bats circled for a while about the spot where the giant tree had recently stood. But there was nothing. Just an absence. Just smoke over the paddocks, settling in the gully. The smell of petrol. Not even a sheep bleating. After a while, when they realised things were no longer in their proper place, the bats fluttered off silently over the paddocks towards the distant river, where there were a few tall trees still standing.

Barry said: 'Birds.'

# BANJO

This story which I will write is not about a great man. But it will be about how he help me get over trying to top myself. This man's name is called Banjo Paterson and I don't see what is so funny about that. I was nothing but a young fellow aged 20 years of age when I met a woman whose name is Margaret. At that time I could not read and I also could not write. I don't know why it seem no one ever tried to teach me before. But I was good with my hands. My Margaret had 4 children which were her children. They are all girls. Margaret and me fell right in love from the start. In time I got to marry this Margaret and the greatest thrill in my life was when she say 'I do' to me inside the registry office. We lived and were v. happy.

Margaret had 2 more children which were my children also. So there were at least 6 children running about all the day and night. Time past or passed. We moved into a real nice house with real cladding on the walls. It was also a v. nice suburb. At that time it was a good place for children to grow up. Apart from some rats in the roof we was v. comfortable.

I worked on Volvo 988 trucks. My job was to fix up Volvo trucks after they had broken down. One day I will go back to this work. My money was v. good. I could work 3 days and nights without sleep to fix a certain Volvo truck. It was dirty work but kind of happy. I loved their grease and the fact that grease is not a secret. Now when I look backwards at what I had, I see I had it all without knowing. I spent more time with trucks than I did with my family. When I lost my happy life I learnt the world was not a good place and I was not a good person in it. I had been married with Margaret about 4 years when it start to happen. My crime which is a v. bad one has to do with the 2 older girls. The youngest 2 were too young. I don't know why it happen that way. It just did. It concern me v. bad. However this is not about my crime which is not hard to imagine. Finally I took the gumption to tell Margaret what was happening with me. With the inside of me. I do not remember the exact words. I telled her because I wanted it to stop. Just to stop. I could not sleep. I begin to hate myself and so I stopped. I work hard. I save money. I stay stopped like that for a year or more but then I begin to hear people whispering about me. Or else stop their whispering when I go in a door. The man at the petrol station would not speak when before he always axed about the weather and what I reckon about the price of fuel or the price of fish. But it was all me. The words in my head, nobody saying anything. The petrol man would not touch my hand when he give back the change. He said everybody has troubles of his own. A funny look in his face. In time I lost my job and started worrying too much, hearing things all the constant.

One day I seed a way of escape. I telled my family we will move to Western Australia and begin a new life. I byed a big

4WD with a powerful donk with lots of grunt and a trailer. So we packed up our boxes. It felt great to tear up the telephone bill and just walk out. The girls did not like to leave their friends or their school but I was their legal guardian and they got to do what I say for their own well being and so on. That was some adventure driving all that way. When we breaked down I fixed us. But everyone got a little bored in the long run. We hit a kangaroo and I had to knock it on the head with a tyre jack. All the girls cry. When we got to Carnarvon I still could not find forgiveness inside or outside of me. So one day, my blackest day, I went to the police and telled them what had happened long ago. V. long ago for I was stopped. I don't know why my head goes like this.

The police thought I was taking the mickey and why did I not just keep quiet, then they took me to see a doctor. The doctor put me to sleep for 4 days which I liked because I did not dream and when I waked up I was 4 days older. Sleep is v. good for you and I had missed it. I stayed in that hospital for several months. I could feel myself growing better, the voices going quiet because I could not dream. The police came to speak to me again. They had spoke to the children and also to Margaret and now said when I was fit for travel I would be extradited back to Victoria. 2 police from Melbourne came and fetched me home. Before we left they stopped by a beach where they taked photos of the purple ocean. In the plane, they cuffed my wrists to my ankles so I could not see the hostess tell us what to do in case of a crash. I kind of hoped the plane would crash but it did not. That was when I first seen Pentridge and Barwon and Loddon.

Jail was all new for me. I know my crime was v. unpopular but also v. common. Everybody give me a bad time considering it. Name calling and spitting started on me. People punching and laying the boot in. Once a knife. The officers giving me grief as well. I had no one to turn to. My cellmate kept trying it on me and when I said 'No' he would lay the boot in. Poured boiling water on me when I was asleep. A deep part of me did not care. One day the inmate who was trying to have sex with me was tipped to another jail. I was on my own now and began to feel better. Whenever there is a lockdown I feel happy. All at peace in my slot. I could see time passing without me having to do much. The other inmates started calling me caveman. A few other names besides like dog and boner and panlicker.

Then Margaret sended me some v. bad letters how I would never see my children which were mine anymore. I did not feel too good. I heard voices in my scone. I made a shiv and slashed up. They give me a few stitches and 2 Panadine then took me to the Assessment cells. So I collected some shoelaces and joined them together. People were happy to give me shoelaces. I was a great joke. People flapping about in loose shoes thinking they were doing the world a favour. The prison psych wrote a letter in her report that I showed no remorse for my crime. After lights out, voices started calling me Rocky and how they going to rape my sister when they get out. I don't tell them I don't have a sister. They were just words but even words get you.

One night with all my shoelaces I tried to hang myself in my cell. Nothing happened but the shoelaces broke and give me a bad burn around my neck. All well and good to laugh. I would vote myself to die but society don't think so. Tried a lot of ways after that to do myself in. Nothing did the trick. So I went back to the locked ward at the hospital on strict protection. More time passes or past. One day out in the yard and this is where I began my story, my ears heard a man reading something. I stood nearby in the sunlight and listened. I seed the razor wire and it is like froth on top of a dirty wave and this is what I heard.

> *They hunted them off the road once more to starve*
> *on the half-mile track*
> *And Saltbush Bill, on the Overland, will many a*
> *time recite*
> *How the best day's work that he ever did was the*
> *day that he lost the fight.*

I axed him to read it all from the start and this man did that for me. Saltbush Bill. When I heard these words I feeled insects prickling my scalp. Afterwards, I feeled alive. Happy and alive and sad all at the same time. It was hard to explain, hard to know inside of me. This man read me more of Banjo Paterson's words. He axed did I want a lend of his book but I told him there was no point as I could not read.

After a while we were called in for muster and lunch. I speaked some more to that man whose name was Pete. Pete and me become good friends. When we go out into the yard on sunny days, Pete would read Banjo Paterson for me. I know now it's not much to speak of but those mornings in the sun mean a great deal to me. In time I told him about my crime and he did not seek to judge me, though he should and maybe he did in his heart. Later they gave me the chance to appeal. Pete said my lagging was v. harsh for what I done and I could cut 2 or 3 years off my top sentence. But I dunno. I am learning here about my mistakes. I am happy to pay and keep paying for them. I am learning about my self. And the self that is not me but who I was. I also dunno if this is justice to get what you expect.

 As this time passes I can see that jail is good for me. It has been necessary. The food is food. I have done my education and have learnt to read and write. Of course, the computer has helped me fix my spelling. I have even been teached about paragraphs; the uses of semi-colons; my past and present tents though I still worry about my future. When I get out, I will go back to fixing trucks if someone will give me a start. Reading and writing will help me locate a job. I will hear no whispers. I will have no dreams. I am doing v. well. I don't know why people laugh when I tell them how Banjo Paterson save my life. Every person has to try and live no matter what they be. Every person's story is different and in time I will be one of them.

# A GOOD BREAK

All this was before he'd applied himself to the learning of First Aid. After the horse had bolted, so to speak.

But for the moment at hand—a heat wave; beachy weather. Half the townspeople sprawled in various stages of leisure and undress. Frisbees in the water; the day hot enough for the dumping margin of the surf to be jumping with swimmers.

Dean had brought the family down to the beach as a kind of littoral gesture to weekend harmony and they'd camped outside the flags (there was no room left between). He glanced with envy at the private shade of a beach umbrella near by. The kids, Gracey and Aaron, ran to the water's edge to begin a game with the waves. Leap, hop, squeal. Shona plonked herself on a towel and pulled a book, no it was a magazine, from her bag. Her eyes squinted at the reflected brightness of the pages. Seagulls strutted about on the sand, puffing their chests out, craning their necks. The shrieking insides of their orange beaks, enough to make someone want to throw a bottle at them. Dean stood keeping an eye on the children.

'Do you think they need any more blockout?'

'What?' asked Shona.

'Do you think they need—'

'You decide, you're their father. I'm having a rest.'

She did not lift her eyes from the page, even though she must have felt the tight grip of crowsfeet about her eyes. Was that fair? Stupid time to come, really, Dean thought. He could have said No, could have insisted that the late afternoon would be a better time. He might have been able to carry on with the work he'd brought home for the weekend. Get ahead. He felt the sun eating through the fabric of his shirt.

Beyond the dumpy waves, surfers danced their dance on the curling breakers further out. Taking advantage of the good break and the tide. Behind him, there was a healthy queue at the ice-cream van in the car park. Dogs. Dean watched the kids now digging a hole in the wet sand; watched them watch it fill with water. He felt the tips of his ears burning. A jogger puffed past, all shiny with sweat. It looked as though he was limping, but that was just the gradient of the sand sloping down to the water. As the waves pulled back from the feet of the bathers, he could see reflected on the shimmering sand, the cliffs at the end of the beach. A sign writer was concocting the first puffy stilts of a message in the sky. Otherwise not a cloud.

'Do you want an ice-cream?' he called to Shona.

'Not yet.'

'Do you think the kids—'

'I don't know. Ask them.'

He turned to the kids, furiously digging their hole, and there, just beyond them, was a punch-up. A struggle in the water between three men. And then suddenly there wasn't. One of the men, a boy really, a youth, called to Dean.

'Give us a hand, mate.'

For a moment Dean considered foisting this plea on to someone else. But there was a particular look he could not name in the boy's eyes, and in that moment there was no one else. Then Gracey stood up to see what was going on.

Two young fellows were holding up an older man between them in buffeting, waist-deep water. His head lolling forward. Dean stepped towards them decisively.

'Go to your mother,' he said, marching past the children.

He admired what ever it was in his tone of voice that made them obey him so swiftly. Dean splashed through the choppy backwash to the young lads who were struggling to keep the older one's head out of the water.

'He was just floating,' said one.

Dean grabbed the legs, which were limp and leaden.

'Up to the sand,' he said.

They were only teenagers. Didn't really know what they were doing.

They staggered out of the water. Between the three of them, the man was as heavy and slack as a sack of lemons. Dean felt mildly shocked at so suddenly having a stranger's feet in his hands. No sooner had they laid him down and rolled him onto his back than the two young lads ran off. Dean looked down at the face before him. He saw the froth and slime at the lips.

Come on mister, snap out of it, he might have thought.

'I don't know how to do this,' he called, as though he were speaking to the figure lying on the sand. Suddenly, a woman dropped to her knees beside him. She tipped the man's head to one side and scooped the white goop out of his mouth with a finger. Then tipping his head back and placing her lips over his she blew heavily into the open jaw.

'Find the xiphoid location,' she said, between breaths.

Dean looked at her stupidly.

'I thought you knew how to do this,' she said.

Dean shook his head. She'd misheard him. He looked at the white slop on her fingers. Then there was another man beside them who seemed to snip some hairs from the hairless chest with his fingers before launching into a fierce barrage of chest pumping. What was that called? Repercussion or something? The woman jerked her face aside as sea water and mucus gushed up into her mouth. She spat on the sand. Returned to breathing.

'Come on mate, you can do it,' said the chest-pumping fellow.

Really, Dean thought, isn't that going a bit far? Surely, after a little rest this chap will spring up and ask what all the fuss is about. He thought this even as he watched the man's face turn blue. Then bluer. There was sand on his eyeball. Dean picked up the fellow's hand and searched for a pulse. The hand was flaccid and cold, the fingers wrinkled from the water.

'I can't find a pulse.'

The others said nothing. Perhaps he hadn't said it at all. From the periphery of his vision, Dean saw several dozen legs gather and mill around them as they worked.

'Does anyone know him?' Dean called out. It was the only thing he could think to do, to try and involve everyone. To his surprise, a voice answered:

'Yeah, he's my uncle.'

Dean glanced up at a face amongst the crowd.

'How old his he?'

'Sixty-two.'

Dean looked at the hard muscles of the stomach; the penis shriveled within the Speedos. Sixty-two! Jeez, he looks fit for sixty-two. He looked at the blue body, the blue hand in his. Even at that moment, the cynic in him wanted to shout: He's your uncle why don't you try and save him? In fact, while we're on about it, where's the bloody lifeguard?

'Can you do this?' asked the man pumping the chest.

'No.'

Surely I'm doing enough—still searching for a pulse and finding none. Should he admit that perhaps he was no good at finding a person's pulse? They turned the man's head to the side again and drained more of the bubbly slop from his mouth. It looked like dishwashing water. This was what he was afraid of, and of not knowing what to do, for despite all the urgency he was afraid. It was like a dream where he should have known and had forgotten everything.

He couldn't believe a face could turn so blue.

After a while someone said, 'Here are the ambos.'

The crowd parted and the uniformed legs of two ambulance officers soon crouched beside them. Calmly they took over. Their uniforms incongruous among the bare legs surrounding them. Thank Christ. Their calm was a deep relief to Dean. Surely now the bloke would be all right. He realised there was no more he could do; that there was probably nothing he had done at all, other than be first on the scene. Apart from the two teenagers, but where were they?

Letting go of the man's hand, he stood and became one of the forest of onlookers.

'There's no carotid or radial pulse,' said the woman who had done the mouth-to-mouth. She knew what she was doing.

'Thank you.'

'He's sixty-two,' Dean thought to add, a voice from the throng.

The ambulance officers opened their box, greased the electroshock pads—whatever they were called—it was just like television.

'Stand clear.'

The body jumped on the sand and lay still. Again. And again. The waves lapping at them. One of the ambulance men told them there was nothing more to see, and the people began to move away. All except the one who had identified the man as his uncle.

Dean went back to Shona and the kids, who had thankfully kept their distance. His hands felt cold. His relief at their calm, also cold.

'What happened, Dad?'

'I don't know, love.'

'Is that man dead?'

'I think so.'

'Will he be all right?'

'I don't know.'

'I've never seen a dead person before.'

He had no idea how much time had passed.

'I don't know what story that nephew is going to tell the aunt.'

Shona put her arm around him, 'Let's get these kids out of the sun.'

They packed their paraphernalia: towels, snorkel, flippers. Warm apples in the bottom of the bag. The message in the sky had blown away.

'Dad can we have an ice-cream?'

'Sure.'

'Can we look in the ambulance?' Its lights flashing in the car park.

They shuffled across the sand. Moving away slowly, as did the other onlookers, from the small scene on the beach. Retrieving their number. And the seagulls and dogs carried their ceaseless activity into the brightness of the afternoon.

# RED SHOES

They want to give me an honorary doctorate. An honorary doctorate when all I want is to lie here and drink tea on the sofa. A long time since I've headed west. Old stomping ground, old wilderness. No more stomping for me, I'm afraid. These fucking feet are fucked. But I get to thinking. West. The turnoff at Wickepin. The weird light. Spears of grass sticking in my bobby socks and braids. Golden dust in my hair. All those ghosts. Running through the wheat, all sweat and sex underneath my pinny. A beauty I was then. A wild creature. Any bloke I fancied. And I fancied them all. I was a mermaid. Look at me now. Prostrate on the couch, a harpooned dugong. Gregor Samsa, that's me, reclining on the fucking commission-built leather catafalque. Look at those feet. Leper's feet. Cut them off at the knees and stick umbrellas in them.

Help me up, Merv, I gotta piss.

* * *

So they want to honour me. Make a big fuss. Want me to clamber up some wooden steps wearing a gown and mortarboard, prance across a rostrum, make a fucking speech. Elocute sweet thankyous into the microphone. I'll give them a speech all right.

'No,' I tell them over the phone, 'I hate flying. Perth is dead for me.'

They'd forgotten all about my forthrightness.

'It's a great accolade,' they say. 'In celebration of your work.'

'Stiff.'

But then I get to thinking; maybe I'm being a bit hasty. I'm not dead yet after all, and maybe Perth has changed for the better. Maybe they've got rid of all the drunks and mad bastards and con men and corruption and ex-husbands, and maybe this and maybe that. In a way, I think it might be kind of nice. Nostalgic. Romantic. On the road again. The last hurrah, instead of lying here rotting away on this fucking couch with a swollen, pouting pillow shaped like Mae West's crimson lips. My lips. You bloody bet. These lips were made for kissing, and that's just what they'll do… Ha! This couch. My final resting place, a library where every book is out of reach and the cracks in the stained glass let in a little whistle of wind.

\* \* \*

Merv packs my ports. Don't forget my red shoes, Merv! I'm not going all that way without my lucky red shoes. This morning, early, he tells me, after insomnia has woken him again, he wandered into the lounge room and found a fox hiding behind the settee. Someone must have left the door open all night. I can picture them together: Merv staring at the fox, the fox staring at Merv; the highway silent, the birds outside just starting to twitch.

'I think it's time you went,' Merv tells me he said to the fox. And the fox went. Here in Faulconbridge. It's a nice story. Fuck knows what it means. Too brief for a play. And who would put on one of my plays? Plays have left me now. All the stories have rolled down hill into the river. Maybe a poem, then. But what about Perth? They want to pay my airfare too, but no thanks. Bloody planes. Bloody airports. Bloody blood pressure. I'm playing hard to get. My inner ear plays up something fierce too on take-off. Bladder at landing. Even driving down the mountains in the back of the hearse shits me to tears. The river like a moat. No. I want to go by train. I want to see the desert, Wickepin. One more time. I want. I want.

So we catch the train. And here we are at Central at the appointed hour. Merv takes care of the ticketing and the bags. Sleeper compartment number such-and-such, with our own foldaway bed and a little stainless steel sink and table and a grimy railway curtain over the window looking out to the grey platform. Merv wheels me up the asphalt like a piece of luggage. Just stare straight ahead, I tell myself. Retain what grace you can. People get out of my way. I hobble up the steps onto the train—goodness the corridors are thin—smell of diesel and rail ballast. I'm holding people up. Why don't they stop staring? Merv clears the corridor before me simply by walking up it. His shoulders touch both walls. Even at eighty, he is a force to be reckoned with. Everyone gets out of his way. Everyone is afraid of what might happen if Merv were to fall on them. Fell on me once and sprained my ankle. 'Merv, get off me foot,' I yelped. He didn't even know. He could clear a room of poets in a flash if he took it into his head. Sometimes I wish he would. And I don't mean with the tureen of mulled wine in the boot of the hearse ladled out into their thirsty cups. He has a great method he employs if he ever has to deal with recalcitrants who want my attention: he simply places a hand on their shoulder, turns them around and sits them down on the floor. They don't get up in a hurry. The trouble is so many people want my attention.

Merv settles me in our compartment, which is a hell of a lot smaller than my library. He takes care of the conductor. Presses a few bribes on him. Eventually we are off. Suburbs flash by, then paddocks, more slowly. Cows stand about like cardboard cutouts of cows. I settle in to our cabin to read through those bloody poems that young up-and-coming-prizewinning suck-hole of a poet has asked me to comment on. Fucked, I should say. Hopeless, I should say. What does he want my opinion for? Why does anyone still want to listen to me? But I won't. I'll be polite and innocuous and lie through my teeth, and people will read it as a considered judgement, as if I know what I'm talking about, and he'll get a grant and stick my comments on the cover of his next book and people will quote me in reviews. I toss the manuscript aside. For Christ's sake, Merv, help me up, I gotta piss.

It's a struggle trying to keep our balance as the *Overlander* rattles across the plains towards Bathurst or somewhere, but he finally squeezes me into the tiny cubicle of the dunny.

'Close the door so I can't hear you,' Merv says. Never could stand to hear the sound of a woman pissing. Could stand a lot of other things though. He could stand more of my behaviour than any other man. Could stand the looks I gave to them, and received, because he knew he was the one and only. Turning awkwardly on my obese axis—there's no other word for it—I manage to click the closet door closed. Mmm, nice alliteration that, although not as nice as the one about the cows, might save it for something, that new poem maybe, about the mad old woman lost in her own house. Click the closet door closed. Click or kick? Closet or corset? Dress hoicked. Bloomers to half-mast. A vicious jolt from the train and I flop onto the seat. Ahh. The sound of a woman pissing. Sorry, Merv. Paper right there. Job well done. Bit of a rest while we're here. Enough of the lady leisurely. Ah, but fuck—I can't get up. My legs are fucked. Come on old girl, of course you can get up. If I... if I... Nngghh... Shit!

'Merv! Merv! I'm stuck.'

And I am. I can't stand up. And I can't open the door. Jesus.

'Dorothy, what is it?' Merv calls.

'I'm stuck.'

Merv tries to open the door but it'll only open six inches before it whacks against my knees. He pushes harder.

'Ow!'

'I'll go and get a conductor.'

'No, no.'

'Why not?'

'I don't want anyone to see me wedged in here with me knickers around me knees.'

I can almost hear Merv cogitating.

'Well, what do you want me to do? You're blocking the door.'

I make a Herculean effort to raise myself, at least to pull my knickers up, but the rocking of the train makes this impossible, and a particularly violent lurch tumbles me first against one wall of the cubicle, then the other. I bang my head.

'Ow.'

I collapse back onto the bowl, slightly stunned.

'Are you all right?'

'No. I'm stuck.'

'Do you want anything?'

'Can't you take the door off or something?'

'The hinges are on the inside.'

'Fuck.'

He's right. Merv doesn't say anything on the other side of the door.

'Are you laughing at me?'

'I'm not that brave.'

Stuck all right. Whose idea was this train anyway? I'm stuck because I'm so fucking fat. And old. I hate growing old. I hate being old. I feel like every vertebra in my spine has been jolted out of the chain. Merv passes in all the cushions and pillows he can find and I pad them around me to stop myself whacking against the walls. In other words, I make myself comfortable. Hours pass. He passes me in a book, but I can't read because of the jolting. I let it fall to the floor, out of sight. The continuous rattling of the wheels is like a dull electric shock, like holding a battery against your tongue. It's not comfortable but after a while you get used to it.

'Do you want this manuscript?'

'Fuck no.'

He passes me small waxpaper cups of water, which I gulp and gulp like some animal at a water hole, and in no bloody time have to piss again. So I piss. Here where I sit. Maybe this is for the best. Maybe I'll die here empty of bladder and pride; all honour gone.

After a while I say, 'Merv, I'm hungry.'

'Do you want me to fetch something from the dining car?'

'Yes.'

'What?'

'Food.'

'What?'

'Anything. Anything. Anything.'

I almost sob.

I hear Merv fossicking about in the compartment and I hear him going out, the door sliding shut behind him. Even when I know he's gone, I still think he's out there, fossicking and I realise I must be delirious. I call. No answer. I call again. No answer. The rattling of the wheels is like dull music, like a battery held against your tongue. I piss. I drink and I piss and I try to read. The transaction is pretty simple. A life's work. This is where devotion to the party gets you. Stuck in a shithouse on the *Overlander*. Dymphna Cusack should be here, not me. That old commo in a tiara, swanning through Moscow in her fur coat. Well Dymphna, did you ever see red shoes like mine? The politburo loved my red shoes. I try not to think about Dymphna for a while, as the music of the train fills me. More hours pass. I think I even doze a little. Merv returns with some railway sandwiches, which he passes in to me.

'What took you so long?'

'I had a cup of tea.'

'Tea! While I'm stuck in here!'

'I've walked the length of the train looking for a lavatory. I can hardly use this one.'

'Sorry.'

'Are you all right?'

'No. My legs hurt. I feel buried alive.'

It's true. I practise scratching my old nails against the door. I try to project the face of several theatre directors I could mention on to the door.

'I can't get you out unless you let me call the conductor.'

'No. What would the vice-chancellor say?'

'Bugger the vice-chancellor.'

Merv has never cared much for vice-chancellors. He goes on in his expedient, male way:

'If I passed you in a screwdriver, do you think you could unscrew the hinges?'

'I don't think I could reach the top ones. Anyway it looks like it needs a special tool.'

'I thought that might be the case.'

'I wish I was fucking dead.'

'You're only saying that.'

'I fucking mean it.'

'I'm trying my best, Dorothy.'

He passes his hand in through the crack. It's a familiar hand with its great thick fingers and calluses from a lifetime of heavy work.

'Have you seen the desert yet?'

'No, Dorothy. It's night.'

'Night? How long have I been in here?'

He wafts his hand about blindly until he finds my face.

'That's my nose.'

'Sorry.'

He strokes my hair and my jowls. He says, 'There, there. Death gives life its shape.'

'What shape?'

'Its meaningless shape.'

It is a great comfort to me, his hand and his words, but it still does not alter the greater fact that I just want to die.

After a while, the rattling of the wheels is no longer like music but more like screaming. I try to sleep. I try to die, propped up by all the cushions Merv has purloined from somewhere. I listen to him snoring. I piss at will, without the inconvenience of having to ask someone to help me up. I've become a baby again. The light burns all night. In the morning he passes in my medicines and food and water and pen and paper in case, he says, you feel inspired.

'Get fucked. I'll give you fucking inspiration.'

I wonder if I have the strength to jab his hand with the biro.

'Do you want your red shoes?'

'No. Fuck off.'

'I can see the desert.'

'What's it like?'

'Flat.'

Strangely, I do try to write. There is nothing else to do, even if it is all delusional. My handwriting is sloppier than usual. Hours pass, and then, presumably, days.

Memories, or perhaps hallucinations, come to me in my fluorescent crypt. Memories of the house at Lambton Downs, of dancing in my red shoes down Darlinghurst Road, of crusty old nuns cursing me to hell. Oh, I was a beauty then. I was a mermaid. I was the embodiment of everything an evil nun should envy. Looks. Lads. Lust. Look at them in their silly wimples and Jesus-shrouds, so ugly they'd make a camel spit. Well, maybe their curses worked. Look at me now. Hell is being stuck in a railway carriage dunny crossing the Nullarbor with only your husband's cracked, familiar hand squeezed in through the door for comfort. All the fluid rushing to your feet making them puff up and burst out of your slippers. Christ, my legs hurt. Tell me again the story of the fox, Merv. Merv, are you there? I wish I could lie down. My arse hurts. Wish I could put my feet up on my lovely couch in my own home, surrounded by my books. Why did we ever leave? I miss the mist and the currawongs. I miss the rowers on the Nepean, even though you only ever glimpse them for a second as you cross the river. If they gave me an honorary doctorate now, in here, I'd bloody well know what to do with it. No, cut the crap. I don't wish for comfort. Not anymore. I only want it to stop. Stop all the camels and flies and heat. Merv, take me home, I wish I was dead, I wish I was fucking dead. There, there, he'll say, strong as an ox, you don't really mean that. Yes, I bloody well do. When I die, Merv, when I finally fucking well die you've got to keep God out of the service. It'll be just like receiving a doctorate. Promise me, no mention of God. Just bury me with some poems and some wattle. I'd like it to be hot. And my red shoes, Merv. Make sure you toss in my red shoes, too. No one wants to see them anymore.

# DRIP, DRIP, DRIP

Etoposide, as is well known, interferes with the function of the unwinding enzyme, preventing the rejoining of DNA. Both single and double strand breaks in DNA can result. Cell death is in proportion to drug concentration and exposure period.

He's lying there like a strange memory of all this. A time before. Like my childhood recollections of him... look, he's lost too much weight, my papa, his skin pale as off milk. Lying there in his bed, wrapped in the crisp concrete of his sheets. I ask him how he's going?

Fine, darl, fine, he says, how's school?

School? I hate his bravery. Do you hear that? I hate how strong you feel you need to be for me. The tea trolley clatters in, then clatters out, as if it is the will of a higher god. He wants nothing. Even the water, he says, tastes like rubber. I look at him. His hair. Even his hair hurts... Alopecia is universal with etoposide...

I have my father's hair. Everybody says so.

Our tyres crunch on hospital gravel. The boom-gate is stuck at a forty-five-degree angle like a salute. Mum hisses we'll never find a park, though I believe we will. Be positive. And we do. Miles away from the door but it's good for you to walk. I count the steps up. I count the passing days. I count the weeks. As the sliding doors part you can smell the smell of cleaning fluids. It's supposed to be a hygienic smell, a nice smell a dry, non-productive cough progressing to shortness of breath with fine (or coarse, in severe cases) basal rates and infiltrates are classical symptoms. Pathologically, a gradual fibrosis of the alveoli occurs, with a decrease of collagen observed in a proportion of the alveolar septae. There is also the smell of sandwiches. I have my father's nose. Everybody says so. In the lift, going up to Oncology, we have to squeeze to one side to make room for a lady lying on a trolley. Her skin, like my daddy's, smells of chemicals.

I am four years old. We are beside a murmuring beach. There are seagulls. I am a little scared of seagulls. The screeching, the colour of their eyes. Chop fat is sizzling on a gas hot plate. Although it's hard being four, it's also good. Dad throws a chop bone and the seagulls pounce on it with a noise like they're murdering each other. One flies off. But I can see that in its greed the bone is sticking sideways in its throat. The gull flaps with the energy of victory. As I watch, it quickly grows tired, up there in the air. Soon its wings give up and it flops like a broken kite down, down into the water where, after it floats for a while like a rag, we forget about it.

Bluebottles are scattered about on the wet sand. Dad nudges one with a stick and warns us never to touch the thin, bright tentacles. Immediately, I want to touch them and when I do I scream, and am given ice-cream for my mouth and vinegar for my fingers.

I'm sitting on my dad's shoulders looking down on his bald patch. The leucocyte nadir occurs five to fifteen days after the dose. His whiskers scratch my thighs. How, oh how did you lose your hair, my dad? It blew, oh it blew off chasing after your mother, he says.

I try to imagine his hair, whether it flies off in a single clump over the waves or whether strands of it float up into the sky's random sewing.

Oh Dad, I'm telling you now, now that even your eyebrows have gone, that was a real dumb joke.

What did you say, darl? I didn't catch that.

Ototoxicity due to cisplatin is well known with tinnitus occurring in nine per cent of patients and symptomatic hearing loss in six per cent. The movements of his head, the slight adjustments of his eyes towards the corners of the ceiling, remind me of a dog cringing at a siren before anyone else has heard. An accident with people dead already, the whole wide mesh of the world carrying on. One lone witness scared of his knowledge.

Etoposide may lower the number of white cells and platelets and as a result the patient should be aware that they will have reduced resistance to infection.

I'll close the window.

I'll pull the curtains.

I'll put up barricades.

I'll block out the sun.

Ah-tchoo!

Any sign of infection, fever, chills, sore throat—any unusual bleeding or bruising—black tarry motions, blood in the urine etcetera, must be reported immediately.

That bag, dripping its clear stuff into him. Up on the stand like the bladder of some poisonous fish they've killed and held aloft. Drip, drip, drip. The stand like a rattle of silver bones; a mannequin in a bridal shop.

My waltzing partner, Dad calls it. Another dumb joke. It even follows him to the dunny. So do the nurses, to examine the infected nugget he struggles to expel. But that's enough. There is the privacy of the old man in the next bed with a tube disappearing into his pyjama pants, trying to rip it out, a nurse holding him down, blood on her tunic. When Dad returns he's stonkered.

Exercise is unnecessary for the healthy and unwise for the sick, he says.

Come on, Dad, this is me. What book did you get that from? But in that short walk from the toilet something has faded from his eyes, and he mutters, Fetch the nurse.

She is too slow and I hate her. When she comes she is as happy as an electric shock.

Cisplatin induces vomiting and nausea in ninety to ninety-five per cent of patients. Poor control of vomiting on previous cycles of therapy increases the incidence and severity of nausea on subsequent cycles.

The nurse is wearing white, and, like the dog at the sound of a bell when he sees the white, he vomits again. It's the white that puts the poison in the bag. Drip, drip, drip. There, there, says nurse, I'll fetch a bowl... That's my father retching, trying to expel a squid from his throat, hiding his face from me.

Sorry, he groans, sorry. Don't Dad, don't protect me anymore. I want to tear the cannula out of his wrist, chuck that silver stand out the window. The nurse gives me a look that says, You'd best go, dear.

A string of squid drools from his lips. He is trying to hide this pale thread from me, as if it is more than the clear core of all this. I would do anything. To help him, I would lick the puke from his chin, like a cow cleaning her calf of the birth slime. If that would help I'd do it. No one will believe that I would do anything. Anything for that chance to help. But I can't. I'm helpless. I'm stuck in the doorway like a whittled stick. The nurse whisks away the kidney dish, studying its contents. The man in the next bed, with the catheter, continues to watch television.

Even that chance to say goodbye is denied me. It's all very complicated. They send for me from school one day, during History, and by the time I get to the ward, every step numbered and frozen in my stone brain, the windows open, the sun shining brightly in, well, everything smells nice and clean and antiseptic... The TV next door is off. Look. I look. I scream get your hands off me. Look. There he is. No one else. It's just as if he's asleep.

# TALES OF ACTION AND ADVENTURE

We're throwing a small dinner to welcome my wife's old friend, Russell, back from his long trek around the globe. The kids are sleeping over so we think we might be able to get in some adult conversation for once. I am cooking. Russell Stanley is Shona's first boyfriend. Someone she has known since high school. His postcards, from various parts of the world, are pinned to the notice board beside the fridge. They have arrived with enviable regularity, adorned with vistas of colourful stamps. Grace, our daughter, is too young or too cool to be interested in stamps, or her mother's old boyfriends.

Shona talks about Russell frequently, relating his news from whatever new part of the planet the latest cards have issued. I can't keep up. Now that I come to think of it, I have never heard Shona say a bad word about Russell. I have heard her say plenty of bad words about other men from her past, but not Russell. It's almost like she still loves him, but that couldn't be correct, because that was years ago and she married me, right? Right? I recall her saying that Russell was distantly related to Stanley, intrepid explorer of Stanley and Dr Livingstone fame. That may be true, but the test of a man's character is relative. We shall see. I have always thought it quaint the way she has managed to maintain friendships from her school days—that sense of shared history. It must be nice. I know no one from my past. They're all ghosts. The past is a haunted place for me. Shona thinks the most intimate knowledge one can have of another person is if you knew them when they wore braces. Shona has perfect teeth now, although she once used to wear braces. I have studied the photos. And there is Russell, right beside her, with braces of his own.

I confess a part of me has been a little jealous of Russell. Of his physique. Of his hair. Of the last seven or eight years when, more often than not, he has been travelling overseas. Lucky beggar. I wonder how he has been able to afford it? It can't have been cheap. Another way of looking at it might be that in the last seven or eight years, he has been out of work more often than not. Alternatively, to claim some solidarity, perhaps Shona is attracted to the outdoorsy, adventurous type, like us.

I am still setting the table when the doorbell rings. Suddenly I am struck by the banality of the sound. Shona is still getting ready. I open the deadlock. Russell is early. The Prodigal boyfriend. There is nothing else for it but to shake his hand.

'Welcome home.'

'Home?' he says, philosophically. I can hear the question mark in his voice: 'Home?'

'Come in. Would you like a beer?'

Russell gives a little shrug.

'No? Wine, then? Or juice?'

'Juice.'

I go into the kitchen, open the fridge, pour a flute of orange juice. The fridge is full of alcohol, but all he wants is juice. When I return Russell is still standing by the front door.

'Would you like me to take my shoes off?'

'No, no. That's fine. Come in. Make yourself at home.'

Russell wipes his feet, then shuffles in and takes off his coat, which I hang by the tall mirror in the hallway. He still cuts a strapping figure. There, that's a sentence from a tale of action and adventure. A strapping figure—despite the tinge of salt and pepper at his temples. He stands at the entrance to the dining room and watches me finish setting the table. The doilies in place. The serviettes. I notice that he peers into his orange juice, examining it closely. A toilet flushes in the distance. In a moment there is a squeal from the far end of the hallway and I take this to mean that Shona has at last spotted her long lost friend. She throws herself into his arms and I find myself counting the seconds of their kiss. She has reverted to a schoolgirl. I think about candles, then dismiss the idea. Candles are too intimate. There are only a few little birthday candles anyway.

I have met Russell before, of course. I couldn't have married Shona without knowing something of her past dalliances, just as she knows mine. Russell's name has always cropped up at her history's most significant moments. I don't know exactly how I feel about this. Once, before I met her, Russell drove Shona to an abortion clinic. Afterwards he took her home and listened to her sob in the shower and made her a cup of tea even though he was not the father. He came to our wedding, of course, and after our daughter was born, a few years later, he gradually faded from our lives. Then, once he had disappeared overseas, the postcards began to arrive. I think it is good for a woman to have male friends, friendships of a platonic, non-threatening nature. Friendships that would be perfectly fine for me to have too.

I have mashed an avocado, mixed with garlic and tomatoes to make guacamole. I have crushed chickpeas and garlic to make my own hummus. I have julienned carrots and celery as instruments to dip and dig into these concoctions. Russell looks at them and sighs. He explains that the jetlag is still catching up with him. He hopes he'll be able to stay awake. Shona seems to find this inordinately funny and giggles. I pour some wine for Shona and, as Russell doesn't appear to be drinking, another juice which again he examines with forensic attention. During this momentary silence the whine of a mosquito is clearly audible. Shona flaps her hand. She hates mosquitoes. I don't mind them because they always bite her and leave me alone. I jump up to put on some music so as to camouflage any future intrusion I fear silence may make into proceedings. Shona apologises for the mosquitoes.

'That's all right,' says Russell. 'Mosquitoes are nothing. In Honduras, near Tegucigalpa, I was bitten by a vampire bat.'

'A vampire bat?'

'I was camping in the jungle and there was a hole in my sock. It bit me on the toe. There was blood everywhere.'

'Weren't you in a tent?'

'There was a hole in that, too.'

'Don't they give you rabies, those things?'

'I don't know.'

'That's amazing,' says Shona.

'Not really. They're very common.'

He takes a celery stick, digs and dips, and pops it into his mouth.

I say, 'I hope you don't mind the garlic in the guacamole, then.'

'No. It's very nice.'

We listen to the music for a moment.

Ambience.

'Shona didn't tell me if you still eat meat or not. We're having lamb, but there's plenty of vegetables as well.'

'Yes, I eat everything,' Russell says. 'In fact, in Brazil I ate a Howler monkey.'

'A Howler monkey?' says Shona, not quite sure if she has heard right.

'Yes, we were travelling overland from Imperatriz and got disoriented in the jungle. We had no food and after a few days my companion, Jacques, shot a monkey.'

'Aren't those things jumping with parasites?' I ask.

'Are they? I don't know.'

'What happened?'

'We cooked it first. It was very tough.'

'Did you get sick?'

'No. My friend got sick. But I was fine.'

'What happened to him?'

'He got better.'

I excuse myself. Duty calls. With industrial strength oven-mitts I fetch hot plates out of the oven. I carve the leg. I serve the slivers. I bring out the main course, garnished with rosemary and mint. Pumpkin. Sweet potato. Lots of spuds in a ceramic bowl that Shona made during her pottery phase. A clichéd Australian meal to welcome back the lonely traveller.

'Careful, the plates are hot.'

Russell chews every mouthful diligently, thoughtfully. I see that candles wouldn't have been amiss. Something I could look at while he is finishing each mouthful. Shona tries to tell him about a holiday we had last Christmas down at Bateman's Bay, but there is not much to tell. Grace stubbed her toe so badly the nail turned black and fell off. Framed photos of the happy, sunburnt children gaze down from the walls. Russell reports that he was stung by a stingray in waters off the coast of Luzon and spent two weeks in a Philippines hospital with the lepers. He offers to show us the scar but Shona declines. She is still eating.

I say, 'I guess you won't have heard about Steve Irwin, then?'

'No,' says Russell. 'Do I know him?'

When he was discharged, Russell continues, he was ordered to rest and recuperate, so he laid up in a beach resort near Tuguegarao. He tells us how the ash from a volcano simmering nearby kept falling into his orange juice and the waiter took twenty minutes to bring a fresh one, even though there was no one else staying at the resort. When it arrived it was brought personally by the manager, who said that all the waiters had evacuated and perhaps sir might like to consider evacuating too. But Russell had already paid up front and was determined to get his money's worth, so he said he would stay put until the volcano erupted if he had to, only it didn't erupt.

Shona says: 'Wow.'

Over dessert, peaches and cream, Russell asks about a mutual school friend of his and Shona's. Shona is sorry to report that the last she had heard, their friend, whose name I forget, broke his ankle falling off a ladder and was on crutches. Russell tells how, while riding a motorbike near Cuzco in the Andes, he hit a condor that hadn't seen him coming and nearly fell into a ravine.

'Didn't it knock you off your bike?' I ask.

'Nearly. It broke the mirror and I lost my deposit. I had bruises the size of dinner plates.'

I clear away the dinner plates and, for the moment, am happy to potter about in the kitchen. I put on the kettle and stack up the dishes. We have a dishwasher, but I am thinking perhaps tonight I will do them by hand. I can hear the music perfectly. When I return with the coffee Russell is telling Shona a story about how he spent six days in a police lock-up in Lushnje in Albania.

'What did you do to deserve that?' I ask.

'Nothing. It was a misunderstanding.'

'I'm afraid there's nothing very exciting about our lives,' says Shona.

'Least of all the coffee,' I add, placing the tray on the table.

'That's all right.'

Russell tells us how, when in Mohitjo, a gypsy touter sold him a quarter ounce of Lebanese hashish. Why? Because it was a good price, and the Australian dollar was so much better than the escudo. It wasn't until he reached the Spanish border a few days later that he remembered it was in his pocket and, as the guards were checking passports, he sat quietly in his train carriage and ate it. What seemed like an hour later, when the guards opened the carriage door, he vomited a foul smelling goop into a plastic bag, which was enough to make the guards, after a cursory glance at his documents, move quickly on. Russell spent the rest of the journey studying the luggage rack overhead, sitting very, very still.

More music.

After coffee, Russell has another. He has several chocolates and several biscuits. I see that I have finished the wine. I think, may as well be hung for a sheep as a lamb, so I open another, even though I will suffer for it tomorrow. I return to the dishes in the kitchen, again leaving the school chums alone to catch up on old times, only I suspect that there are not too many old times being chewed over. There seems to be a big loud silence coming from the dining room. Like flat champagne. I clean everything in the kitchen. In fact, I give it a thorough scrubbing. I sweep the floor. I clean the oven. I change the music a few times. I overhear Russell say, in response to Shona's question, that one of the things he has learnt in his travels is that the native Inuits from Inuvik in Canada always take a long time over their meals so as to strengthen the social and familial bonds. They have a word: *sunasorpok*, which means to clean up the food left unfinished by others. I am glad I have removed the plates—there was only fat left on mine. A part of me wonders if Russell is making this up, if he has, in fact, been lying. I have never really swallowed the Stanley-Livingstone story. So I sneak into the study and quickly Google Canadian Inuit eating rituals. This search yields zero results: *Did you mean Canadian Restaurants?* Such a dead end proves nothing, which merely reinforces my more general suspicion that Google is a great way to prove nothing. I'll have to take Russell's word for it.

When I eventually return, Russell is sitting with his hands around his coffee mug, as if it is still warm. The school chums have run out of conversation. The old flame is flickering. Shona is looking decidedly weary and Russell looks as though he does not want to leave, ever. I see he has kicked his boots off. The couch is looking far too comfortable. Thank goodness he hasn't been drinking. I sit down beside Shona and give an enormous, prefabricated yawn. Russell tells us how he was robbed at gunpoint in Rybinsk but only had about thirty roubles in his pocket at the time, so everything worked out for the best. I realise, with the aid of my peripheral vision, something Russell has not—that Shona has fallen asleep. She gives a little, soft snore.

'My God, you've had some adventures, Russell,' I eventually say. 'In these exotic places. I don't know where half of them are.'

'Not really,' he replies. 'It was all pretty boring.'

The sound of my laughter wakes Shona with a start. The dream-word she drags out of her snooze is: *Curriculum*.

She's clearly got other things on her mind.

'Oh Russell, I'm sorry. I'm afraid I'm going to have to go to bed.'

'Me too,' I add. 'We've both got work tomorrow.'

'Oh,' says Russell. 'Bummer.'

Shona clambers to her feet and shows him to the door. He does not look at the photos on the walls.

'Don't forget your coat.'

'Did I tell you about the time I forgot my coat in Keflavik in Iceland? It's the most expensive place I've ever—'

'Perhaps next time.'

'Oh... okay... when?'

'I'll give you a ring.'

Russell puts on his coat and, reluctantly, leaves. We listen to his footsteps, but there is no sound of an engine from out on the quiet street. I wonder if he is out there, waiting for us to change our minds and invite him back in. I clear away the coffee mugs. The kitchen is sparkling. I am so good. I go to the bathroom and brush my teeth. I do it with my left hand so as to stimulate alternative neural pathways and thus avert the potential onset of dementia. While I do this I stand on one foot, like a stork, for thirty seconds at a time so that my body will retain its physical memory of balance and not leave me bereft when I am older. I am thinking ahead. Shona comes in behind me. Like the children, she no longer asks what I am doing. She already has on her nightie. She hoists it and sits on the toilet unselfconsciously.

'You cooked a lovely meal,' she says, 'my dear, sweet adventurer.'

'Me? It's all I can do to get the car started in the morning.'

She must have looked adorable with braces. After she washes her hands, she gives me a sleepy hug, her mouth humming against my neck, which I take to be a manifestation of her love, love that is not humming against the neck of her old school flame.

'Did you enjoy seeing your pal?'

'What a dreary man,' she says, yawning again, as content as I've seen her.

# ACKNOWLEDGEMENTS

These stories have previously appeared, sometimes in slightly different forms, in the following journals and magazines. My thanks to their editors. 'Red Shoes' co-winner, *Patricia Hackett Prize*, 2008 and 'Tales of Action and Adventure' highly commended, *Shoalhaven Short Story Award*, 2009.

'Bulldozer', *Muse*, Oct, 1996
'Loaded Dice', *Siglo #6*, 1996
'Drip, Drip, Drip' *Australian Short Stories #64*, 1998
'Banjo' *Southerly Vol 60 #2*, 2000
'A Good Break', *Overland #171*, 2003
'Lovely Outing', *Meanjin Vol 64 #3*, 2005
'Bridie', *Wet Ink #6*, 2006
'The Ingot', *Island #109*, 2007
'Stealth', *The Big Issue #269*, 2007
'White Light', *Heat #13*, 2007
'Red Shoes',*Westerly Vol 53*, 2008
'Iago' *New Australian Stories 1*, 2009
'Tales of Action and Adventure' *New Australian Stories 2*, 2010
'Beneath the Figs' *Going Down Swinging #30*, 2010 and also in *The Best Australian Stories*, 2011
'The Isthmus', *Southerly Vol 71 #3*, 2011
'Ping-Pong Principle', *Review of Australian Fiction Vol3 # 3*, 2012

# SINGLE AUTHOR

In this short story collection, travellers on highways and trains are preoccupied with the lives of the dead, with lost children or with parents. A woman searches a suburban deadland for her missing mother. A rural family struggles on a land that fails to sustain them. A young man's attempt to leave the strictures of family life ends in violence.

*'A talent to watch.'*
WALTER MASON

In these seventeen stories, Melbourne writer, Mary Manning, looks at the ways people are shaped, or damaged, by their circumstances. The results may sometimes be humorous, sometimes tragic. Whether set on a tram, along a highway or on an outback road?it is the journey, the characters and the telling of the tale that will capture your attention.

*'Tart, tight and compulsively readable.'*
PADDY O'REILLY

What makes a man? In this collection of short stories, Pierz Newton John moves through the full range of masculine experience, with an openness not afraid to show men at their most lonely, sexual, loving, sometimes vulnerable, sometimes abusive.

*'A startling collection…sly humour and memorable characters.'*
CHRIS WOMERSLEY

# COLLECTIONS

This entertaining collection includes a romp of a novella as well as short stories and micro fictions all set in and around contemporary Melbourne. Sometimes serious, sometimes seriously playful –always written in breathtakingly beautiful prose.

*"Be careful. These stories might cut you.'*
RYAN O'NEILL

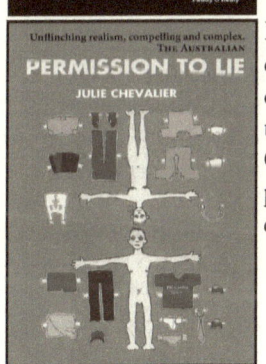

In *Permission to Lie*, Julie Chevalier casts a curious eye into many different worlds. Her characters ride the citybound bus route, spend the night in a nudist colony and wait tables. Quirky and beautifully-written, these stories provide insights that ring with integrity and compassion.

*'A new voice in Australian fiction, wry, gritty, knowing and true.'*
FIONA MCGREGOR

'New kids on the block SPINELESS WONDERS steadily put out edgy and interesting single-author collections.'
Jennifer Mills, fiction editor, *OVERLAND*

# ANTHOLOGIES

In this anthology, our editor, Angela Meyer, pays tribute to the undeniable cultural influence that American TV programs such as Twilight Zone and Outer Limits have had on our lives 'down under'.

'These TV dramas,' Meyer says, ' were often metaphors for equality, justice, the nuclear threat and more. Though they were just as often pure, spooky fun.'

Due for release Dec 2013

If you like your genres with a bit of edge, you'll love this diverse collection of stories from Spineless Wonders. Features award-winning writers such as Ryan O'Neill, Jen Mills, Andy Kissane, Louise Swinn, Julie Chevalier, A.S. Patric and Kim Westwood as well as stories chosen by Sophie Cunningham in the inaugural Carmel Bird Short Fiction Award.

*'Quality short fiction, packed with surprises. Prepare to be transported.'* Marion Halligan

# THE CARMEL BIRD
# SHORT FICTION AWARD

# PROSE POEM & MICROFICTION

What do our best wordsmiths have to say about Australian icons? This anthology takes a fresh look at everything from the HIH collapse to crocs, Margaret Olley, bush burials and the ABC. We visit a post-apocalyptic Opera House and spend Saturday night in downtown Byron Bay.

*'A celebration of the many things Australia can mean to us.'*

NEWTOWN REVIEW OF BOOKS

Here are short and clever pieces by thirty contemporary Australian writers on topics ranging from the eroticism of mash potato, parenting as magic realism and a tongue-in-cheek history of the Cyclops bicycle. Includes award-winning writers Michael Farrell, Keri Glastonbury, Judith Beveridge, Peter Boyle, Kent MacCarter, Erin Gough and Charles D'Anastasi.

*'A treasure trove.'* READINGS MONTHLY

# THE joanne burns AWARD

# *Dear Writer Revisited*

The Classic Guide to Writing Fiction

**Dear Writer**
...revisited...

**CARMEL BIRD**

This book about writing and the imagination is essential reading for any writer, emerging or experienced. Re-released with new material and updated advice for the Twenty-first Century writer.

"Carmel Bird has updated her brilliant guide to those who are perplexed by writing. *Dear Writer Revisited* is a dazzling, humane and witty book which will be enlightening for anyone who picks it up, however experienced she or he may be. This is a classic account of how to write. I know of nothing that equals it."

PETER CRAVEN

'I first read *Dear Writer* as a nervy, secretive scribbler-in-journals 20 years ago. Reading this revised version I'm struck again by its practical generosity on technical matters - but am also inspired by the deeper, more complex conversations I think I missed in those early readings: about courage, about the urgency and mystery and self-discovery of the writing process. *Dear Writer Revisited* may masquerade – convincingly – as a book for beginners, but its lessons are mature and wise.'

—CHARLOTTE WOOD
THE WRITER'S ROOM INTERVIEWS

# EARWORMS

Earworms are those songs with unforgettable hooks that get stuck in your head but Spineless Wonders brings you short Australian earworms—stories by award-winning writers that you definitely won't want to forget.

Stuck in a queue? Don't stress. You can listen to our selection of funny, political and thought-provoking prose poems and microfiction from our anthology, Small Wonder.

Got a pile of washing-up or ironing to do? Housework's not a chore when you can listen to short fiction from our anthology, Escape.

Commuting every day? Traffic jams are not a problem when you can listen to the latest in contemporary short fiction from Spineless Wonders.

Prices range from $0.99 to $2.99. Gift vouchers available. Listen to our audio trailers at

www.shortaustralianstories.com.au/audio